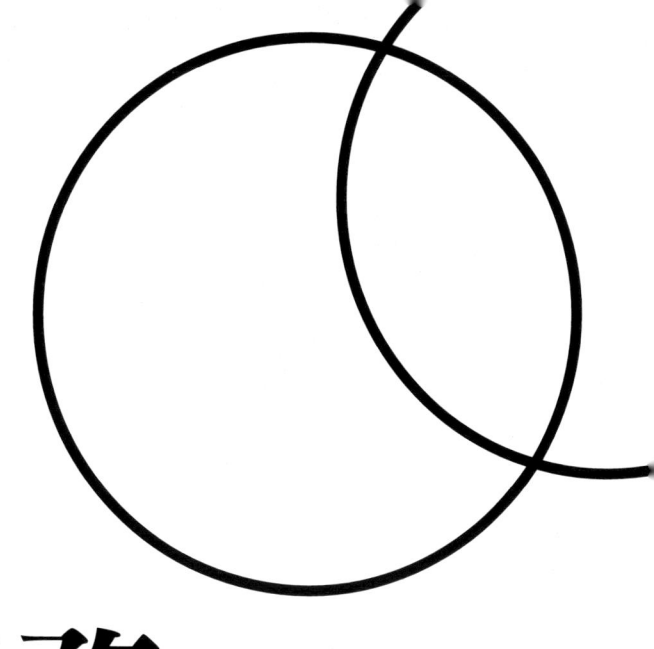

酒店服務
英語簡明教程

覃始龍 主編

財經錢線

前言

　　全書以酒店服務的前廳、客房、餐飲、會務以及康樂五大服務領域為主線，分成五大對應章節。每章節精心選取各個部門的常用英語服務情境，分成若干個相對獨立的單元。每個單元由背景知識、若干短對話、中文翻譯、單詞和短語、練習題等部分組成。針對高職學生的英語基礎和學習能力實際，本書內容以「簡明」為主。在詞彙、句式、篇章長度等方面，均考慮到高職學生的實際情況，化難為簡，使學生容易上手，方便自學，能克服詞彙和語法障礙。各章節和單元的內容之間既互相獨立，又適當重複語言點。學習者不一定要從第一頁開始學習，可以選擇全書的任何章節開始學習，減輕心理負擔，從而能夠在主動操練中達到對語言知識的掌握和熟記。本書大部分的練習題均在書後提供了參考答案。附錄部分提供了關於酒店評論的泛讀材料，可供學習者加深對酒店服務英語的瞭解和熟練掌握。

　　由於編者水準有限，除了平時在教學過程中形成的累積之外，在編寫過程中還參考了大量的中外文獻和網路素材。在此，一併對引用文獻的著作權人表示衷心的感謝！對於本書存在的不足之處，懇請各位專家、學者和讀者不吝批評指正，我們會在再版時修正。

編者

目錄

Chapter One　Front Office 前廳部 ·· (001)
　　Unit 1　Room Reservation　客房預訂 ································· (001)
　　Unit 2　Reception　登記入住 ··· (010)
　　Unit 3　Bell Service　應接服務 ·· (016)
　　Unit 4　Telephone Operator　總機服務 ······························· (025)
　　Unit 5　Business Center　商務中心 ····································· (032)
　　Unit 6　Complaints　處理投訴 ·· (041)
　　Unit 7　Check-out　結帳退房 ··· (048)

Chapter Two　Housekeeping 客房部 ······································ (055)
　　Unit 1　Showing Room　介紹客房 ······································· (055)
　　Unit 2　Cleaning Room　客房清理 ······································· (063)
　　Unit 3　Room Service　送餐服務 ··· (070)
　　Unit 4　Laundry Service　洗衣服務 ····································· (077)
　　Unit 5　Emergencies　突發事件 ··· (083)
　　Unit 6　Other Housekeeping Service　客房其他服務 ············· (091)

Chapter Three　Food and Beverage 餐飲部 ···························· (097)
　　Unit 1　Reservation　預訂餐臺 ··· (097)
　　Unit 2　Receiving Guests　迎客服務 ···································· (103)
　　Unit 3　Western Food　西餐服務 ··· (109)
　　Unit 4　Chinese Food　中餐服務 ··· (115)
　　Unit 5　At the Bar　酒吧服務 ··· (123)

Chapter Four　Conferences 會務部 ………………………………………………（132）

Chapter Five　Health & Recreation Service 康樂部 ……………………………（142）
　　Unit 1　At the Recreation Center　健身中心 …………………………………（142）
　　Unit 2　At the Barbers & Beauty Salon　美容美髮廳 …………………………（147）

參考答案 …………………………………………………………………………………（155）

Appendix：Extended Reading Materials on Hotel Reviews
　　　　　（附錄：關於酒店評論的泛讀材料）………………………………………（164）

Chapter One　Front Office 前廳部

Unit 1　Room Reservation　客房預訂

Background（背景知識）

The reservationist responds to communications from guests, travel agents, and referral networks concerning reservations arriving by mail, telephone, telex, cable, fax, or through a central reservation system. He creates and maintains reservation records—usually by date of arrival and alphabetical listing. He prepares letters of confirmation and promptly processes any cancellations and modifications.

Additional duties may include preparing the list of expected arrivals for the front office, assisting in preregistration activities when appropriate, and processing advance reservation deposits.

Situational dialogues（情景對話）

Dialogue 1

R—Reservationist　G—Guest

R: Good morning, Horizon Hotel. What can I do for you?

G: Yes, I'd like to reserve a double room with a private bath.

R: Thank you, sir. From which date and how long will you be staying?

G: From September 11th to 15th.

R: Would you hold the line, please? I'll check our vacancies for those days. We happen to have some double rooms with bath available. The room rate is 680 yuan per night.

G: That is fine. Please hold it for me. This is Phillips and my number is 89215740.

R: Of course, Mr. Phillips. I'll have the room ready for you. Thanks for your calling. We are looking forward to your arrival on September 11th.

G: Thanks, and good bye.

Translation（譯文）

R——預訂員　G——客人

R：早上好，地平線酒店。我能為您做什麼？

G：是的，我想預訂一個帶浴室的雙人間。

R：謝謝您，先生。從哪天開始，住多久？

G：從9月11日到15日。

R：請您不要掛斷好嗎？我將檢查我們的空房。我們有帶浴室的雙人房。房費是每晚680元。

G：那很好。請為我保留此房。我是菲利蒲，我的電話號碼是89215740。

R：沒問題，菲利蒲先生。我會為您準備好房間。謝謝您的來電。我們期待9月11日您的到來。

G：謝謝，再見。

Words and expressions（單詞和短語）

reserve 預訂

double room 大床房

private 私人的

bath 浴室

vacancy 空房

available 可用的

room rate 房費

hold the line 別掛電話

looking forward to 期待

arrival 到達

Dialogue 2

R—Reservationist　G—Guest

R：Good afternoon, Room Reservations. May I help you?

G：Good afternoon. This is Johnson calling from Britain. I'd like to book a twin room from October 1st to 7th, please.

R：That's fine, sir. A twin room from October 1st to 7th, with street view or sea view?

G：What's the price difference?

R：A twin room with street view is 80 dollars per night; one with sea view is 90 dollars per night.

G：I think I'll take the one with sea view then.

R：Ok, Mr. Johnson. Your room will be ready at noon on your arrival day.

Translation（譯文）

R——預訂員　G——客人

R：下午好，預訂部。有什麼可以幫您嗎？

G：下午好。我是約翰遜，從英國打來電話。我想訂一個雙床房，時間是從10月1日到7日。謝謝。

R：好的，先生。從10月1日到7日的雙床房。您喜歡街景房還是海景房呢？

G：兩種房間的價格有什麼不同？

R：街景的雙床房每晚80美元，海景的是每晚90美元。

G：我覺得還是要海景的吧。

R：好的，約翰遜先生。您的房間在到達當天中午就可以準備好了。

Words and expressions（單詞和短語）

reservation 預定

twin room 雙床間

October 十月

view 景色

difference 不同

price 價格

per night 每晚

Dialogue 3

R—Reservationist　G—Guest

R：Thank you for your waiting, sir. We do have a deluxe suite at US＄268 per night from October 1st to 6th. Will that be fine?

G：OK. I'll take that.

R：May I have your name and your telephone number, please?

G：Yes, my name is Paul Simon and my cell phone number is 13756734590.

R：Mr. Paul Simon, and your cell phone number is 13756734590… Excuse me, how do you spell your family name?

G：It's S-I-M-O-N.

Translation（譯文）

R——預訂員　G——客人

R：讓您久等了，先生。10月1日至6日期間，我們有一個豪華套房，每晚268美元，您覺得可以嗎？

G：好的。我就要這間。

R：麻煩告知您的名字和電話號碼，好嗎？

G：好的，我叫保羅・西蒙，手機號碼是13756734590。

R：保羅・西蒙先生，您的手機號碼是13756734590……對不起，怎麼拼寫您的姓氏呢？

G：是 S-I-M-O-N。

Words and expressions（單詞和短語）

deluxe 高級的

suite 套房

cell phone 手機

spell 拼寫

family name 姓

Dialogue 4

R—Reservationist G—Guest

R: Thank you, Mr. Simon. For the unguaranteed reservation, we can only hold the room by 6:00 p.m., because it is the peak season now. If you make a guaranteed reservation, we can hold the room overnight. Would you like to make a guaranteed reservation by credit card?

G: No, I will be there before then.

R: Thank you very much, Mr. Simon. That's all settled then and we look forward to seeing you on Friday.

G: Thank you and goodbye.

R: Goodbye.

Translation（譯文）

R——預訂員 G——客人

R：謝謝，西蒙先生。對於無擔保預訂，我們只能保留房間到下午6點，因為現在是旺季。如果您進行擔保預定，我們可以為您整夜保留房間。您願意用信用卡來擔保預定嗎？

G：不，我將在那時之前抵達。

R：非常感謝，西蒙先生。那就全辦妥了，我們期待周五見到您。

G：謝謝你，再見。

R：再見。

Words and expressions（單詞和短語）

guarantee 擔保

peak season 旺季
overnight 過夜
credit card 信用卡
settle 解決

Dialogue 5

R—Reservationist   G—Guest

G: Good morning. I'd like to make a reservation. What kinds of rooms do you have?

R: We have single rooms, double rooms, triple rooms and suites like junior suites, deluxe suites, presidential suites, and business suites.

G: Well, I'd like to book a single room from October 1st to the 10th.

R: Wait a moment, please. I'm sorry, sir. The single rooms are fully booked for those dates, but we still have double rooms. Would you like to have one?

G: No, thank you. How about business suites?

R: Let me see. We still have five business suites available.

G: What's the rate for one?

R: It's 550 yuan a day, including service and breakfast.

G: OK. I'll have one.

R: May I have your name, please?

G: Stephen Lee.

R: Well, Mr. Lee, we look forward to your arrival.

Translation（譯文）

R——預訂員　G——客人

G：早上好。我想訂房。你們有什麼樣的房間呢?

R：我們有單人房、雙人房、三人房和套房，比如普通套房、豪華套房、總統套房及商務套房等。

G：嗯，我想訂一間從10月1日到10日的單人房。

R：請稍等。我很抱歉，先生，這些日期的單人房都訂滿了，但是我們還有雙人間，您想訂一間嗎?

G：不用了，謝謝。商務套房怎麼樣?

R：讓我看看。我們還有五個空餘的商務套房。

G：一套租金是多少?

R：每天550元，包括服務費和早餐。

G：好的。我要訂一套。

R：請告訴我您的名字，好嗎？
G：斯蒂芬·李。
R：好的，李先生，我們期待著您的光臨。

Words and expressions（單詞和短語）

single room 單人房
triple room 三人房
junior suite 普通套房
deluxe suite 高級套房
presidential suite 總統套房
business suite 商務套房
fully booked 訂滿
include 包含
breakfast 早餐
service 服務

Dialogue 6

Translation（譯文）

R—Reservationist G—Guest

R: Good morning, Horizon Hotel. Can I help you?

G: I'd like to reserve 16 standard rooms with your hotel for some visiting scholars.

R: What dates would you like them?

G: From 15th to 21st of May.

R: Just a moment, please. Let me check the reservation list. I'm very sorry. We only have 14 standard rooms available on May 15th. However, from 16th to 22nd, we have adequate standard rooms for you. Can you change the date of arrival to 16th?

G: Oh, no, we can't. Because these visiting scholars will attend a very important international academic exchange activity in Beijing.

R: We also have some junior suites available on the 15th. The price of a junior suite is $30 more than that of a standard room, and we have a special rate for group reservation for junior suites.

G: How much is a standard room per night? And how much discount do you have for the junior suites?

R: $180. We will give you 10% off for the reservation of the junior suites.

G: That's great. I'd like to book 14 standard rooms and two junior suites altogether. My name is Bryan Tan, and my telephone number is 15825639871.

R: Thank you, Mr. Tan. You have booked 14 standard rooms and two junior suites from May 15th to the 21st. And your telephone number is 15825639871.

G: That's right. Thank you.

R: You are welcome. If there is anything changeable, please call me. Goodbye.

Translation（譯文）

R——預訂員　G——客人

R：早上好，地平線飯店。需要幫忙嗎？

G：我想在貴酒店為一些訪問學者訂16個標準間。

R：什麼日期呢？

G：從5月15日至21日。

R：請稍等，讓我查一下預訂列表。很抱歉，5月15日我們只有14個標準間可用。不過，從16日到22日我們有足夠的標準間。您能把抵達日期改到16日嗎？

G：哦，不。我們不能，因為這些訪問學者將在北京出席一個非常重要的國際學術交流活動。

R：15日我們也有一些普通套房。普通套房的價格比標準間貴30美元。我們對團體預訂的普通套房有特價。

G：一個標準間每晚多少錢？普通套房多少折扣呢？

R：180美元。預訂普通套房，我們將給您10%的折扣。

G：那太好了。我想訂14個標準房間和兩個普通套房。我的名字叫布萊恩·譚，我的電話號碼是15825639871。

R：謝謝您，譚先生。您已經訂了從5月15到21日的14個標準間和兩個普通套房。您的電話號碼是15825639871。

G：沒錯。謝謝你！

R：不客氣。如果有任何變動，請給我致電。再會。

Words and expressions（單詞和短語）

standard room 標準間

visit 訪問

scholar 學者

list 清單

adequate 足夠的

change 更換

attend 出席

important 重要的

international 國際的
academic 學術的
exchange 交流
special rate 特價
group reservation 團體預訂
discount 折扣
changeable 易變的

Exercises（練習題）

I. Complete the sentences.（補全句子）

1. I'd like to book a _____ room for Tuesday next week.
下周二我想訂一個雙人房。

2. What's the price _____?
兩種房間的價格有什麼不同？

3. A double room with a _____ view is 140 dollars per night.
一間帶湖景雙人房每晚 140 美元。

4. I think I'll _____ the one with a lake view then.
我想我還是要湖景的吧。

5. How _____ will you be staying?
您打算住多久？

6. We'll be _____ Sunday morning.
我們將在星期天上午離開。

7. And we look forward _____ seeing you next Tuesday.
我們盼望下周二見到您。

8. I'd like to book a single room _____ from the afternoon of October 4 to the morning of October 10.
我想訂一個帶洗澡間的單人房間，10 月 4 日下午到 10 月 10 日上午用。

9. We do have a single room _____ for those dates.
我們確實有一個單間，在這段時間可以用。

10. What is the room _____, please?
請問房費多少？

11. The current rate is ＄50 _____ night.
現行房費是 50 美元一天。

12. What services come _____ that?

這個價格包括哪些服務項目呢？

13. That _____ not bad at all. I'll take it.
聽起來還不錯。這個房間我要了。

14. By the way, I'd like a quiet room away from the street if _____.
順便說一下，如果有可能我想要一個不臨街的安靜房間。

15. How many guests will there be in your _____?
您一行有多少人？

16. What time do you expect to _____?
您打算什麼時間到達？

17. What kind of room would you _____?
您想要什麼樣的房間？

18. A standard room 850 RMB per night, with 10% tax and a 10%_____ charge.
標準間每晚850元人民幣，外加10%的稅金和10%的服務費。

19. I'm afraid we have no twin room available. Would you mind a _____ instead？我們恐怕沒有空餘的雙床間了。您介意改訂套間嗎？

20. We'll book you into a room with a _____ from the 6th to 8th this month.
我們會為您在本月的6日到8日預訂一間有陽臺的房間。

21. In whose name was the _____ made?
您的預訂是用誰的名字？

22. We'll _____ the reservation for you.
我們會為您取消此次預訂的。

23. Should I ask a _____ to take the luggage to your room?
需要我讓行李生幫您把行李送到房間嗎？

II. Make a dialogue according to the following situation.（創作情景對話）

顧客B打來訂房電話，前臺服務員A接聽。B想要預訂5月6號到5月9號共三晚的兩個標準間和一間套房。但是現在是旅遊旺季，套房已經全部預訂出去。B決定要三個標準間。房價是130美元加上百分之十五的服務費和稅金。B希望酒店能提供接機服務。A請B留下了航班號及抵達時間。請根據以上情景，創作一篇不少於100個單詞的英文對話。

Unit 2　Reception　登記入住

Background（背景知識）

Hotels are busy and demanding but with great fun! As the hotel receptionist, it is important to realize that you are the face of that hotel: You're the first person to greet guests as they arrive, you're the person they will come to if they have any problems and you're the first person they speak to on the phone.

Guests in person are very important and should always be acknowledged. There is nothing worse than waiting to be spoken to. If you're on the phone or dealing with someone else, a nod or smile of acknowledgement is all that is needed, but you could follow with a cheerful「I'll be with you in a moment」.

When someone walks into the reception, you should always stand up, if you're not standing already. Shake their hands if appropriate and smile. People want to be welcomed, and made to feel comfortable when they're staying away from home and as the receptionist, you set the tone for the rest of the stay. People remember impeccable service and they love it.

Situational dialogues（情景對話）

Dialogue 1

R—Receptionist　G—guest

R: Good morning, sir. What can I do for you?

G: Good morning. I have a reservation for a single room with bath here.

R: May I have your name, please?

G: Darius Robertson.

R: Just a moment, please, sir. Yes, we do have a reservation for you, Mr. Robertson. Would you please fill out this registration form?

G: What should I fill in under「Room Number」?

R: You can just skip that. I will put in the room number for you later on.

G: Here you are. I think I've filled in everything.

R: Let me see... name, address, nationality, passport number, visa number, signature and date of departure. Oh, you forgot to put in the date of departure. Let me fill it in for you. You are leaving on...

G：October 24.

R：Now everything is in order. Here is your room card, Mr. Robertson. Your room number is 1420. Please take good care of your room card. You need to show it when you sign for your meals and drinks in the restaurants and bars.

G：OK, I will.

R：And now if you are ready, I will call the bellboy to take you to your room.

G：Yes, I'm ready. Thank you.

R：I hope you enjoy your stay with us.

Translation（譯文）

R——接待員　G——客人

R：早上好，先生。我能為您做什麼？

G：早上好。我在這兒預訂了一個帶浴室的單人房。

R：能告訴我您的名字嗎？

G：大流士·羅伯遜。

R：請稍等，先生。是的，我們有您預訂的房間，羅伯遜先生。請您填寫這張登記表好嗎？

G：在「房間號」這一欄我該怎麼填呢？

R：您可以直接跳過。我稍後給您填上房間號。

G：給您，我想我填完了。

R：讓我看看……姓名、地址、國籍、護照號、簽證號、簽名和離店日期。哦，您忘了把離店日期填上。我來幫您填寫。您離店日期是……

G：10月24日。

R：現在一切辦妥了。羅伯遜先生，這是您的房卡。您的房號是1420。請保管好您的房卡。您在餐廳和酒吧簽單享用食物和飲料時需要出示它。

G：好，我會的。

R：如果您準備好了，我就叫行李員帶您去房間。

G：是的，我準備好了。謝謝你！

R：祝您住店愉快！

Words and expressions（單詞和短語）

reception 接待

reservation 預定

bath 浴室

registration 入住登記

form 表格

fill in 填寫

skip 跳過

later on 稍後

address 地址

nationality 國籍

passport 護照

visa 簽證

signature 簽名

departure 離開

put in 填入

in order 辦妥

room card 房卡

take good care of 小心拿好

sign 簽名

meal 一餐（頓）飯

restaurant 餐廳

bar 酒吧

bellboy 行李員

Dialogue 2

R—Receptionist   G—Guest

R: Good afternoon, Mr. Robertson. It's nice to have you with us again.

G: Thank you. It's nice to be back in Guangzhou even if I am staying here for only three days.

R: How was your flight from San Francisco, Mr. Robertson?

G: Fine, thank you. I have no reservation with your hotel this time. I want the suite facing south where I stayed last time.

R: Please wait a moment. Unfortunately, the suite was booked this morning. But we have a suite available facing the lake. The room rate is just the same as the one you stayed in last time.

G: OK, I will take it.

R: How would you like to pay, by credit card?

G: With US dollars traveler's check, I think.

R: Your suite is on the ninth floor, room 905. Here is your key card. Do you need a porter, Mr. Robertson?

G: It is not necessary. Thank you very much.

R: It's my pleasure to serve you again. Hope you will enjoy your suite.

Translation（譯文）

R——接待員　G——客人

R：羅伯遜先生，下午好。很高興您能再次下榻本酒店。

G：謝謝你。很高興回到廣州，雖然我只在這裡呆三天。

R：您從舊金山過來的航班，一路順利嗎，羅伯遜先生？

G：很好，謝謝。這次我沒有預訂。我想要我上次住過的那個朝南的套間。

R：請稍等。不巧的是，那個套間今天早上被別人訂了。但是我們有一個面朝湖泊的套間。房價和您上次那間是一樣的。

G：好吧，我就要這間吧。

R：您想怎樣付帳，用信用卡嗎？

G：用美元旅行支票吧。

R：您的套間在9樓，905房間。這是您的鑰匙卡。你需要行李員嗎，羅伯遜先生？

G：不必了。非常感謝。

R：很榮幸為您服務。希望您能喜歡該套間。

Words and expressions（單詞和短語）

flight 航班；飛行

facing south 朝南

unfortunately 不幸地

lake 湖

traveler's check 旅行支票

porter 行李員

necessary 必需的

pleasure 愉快

serve 招待

Dialogue 3

R—Receptionist　G—Guest

G: Hello, my name is Jane Paris. I'd like to check in.

R: Wait a minute, please. Let me check it. Yes, madam, you have reserved a single room for a week.

G: That's right.

R: May I see your passport and visa?

G: Of course.

R: Thank you. Your room number is 1712. Here is the key.

G: Good.

R: And we need $100 deposit for the key. You can get it back when you leave.

G: Here you are.

R: Thank you. And do you mind leaving your passport and visa here for an hour or so? We need to make a copy of them for our records.

G: No.

R: Here is your receipt for your deposit. Please keep it.

G: Thank you.

R: You are welcome. Enjoy your stay here.

Translation（譯文）

R——接待員　G——客人

G：你好，我叫簡·帕里斯。我想辦理入住。

R：請稍等。我來核對一下。是的，女士，您預定了一個單人間，為期一個星期。

G：沒錯。

R：我可以看一下您的護照和簽證嗎？

G：當然。

R：謝謝。您的房號是1712。這裡是鑰匙。

G：好的。

R：我們需要收100元作為鑰匙的押金。退房的時候可以退回給您。

G：給你。

R：謝謝。您介意把護照和簽證留在這裡一個小時左右嗎？我們需要複印作為記錄。

G：不介意。

R：這是您的押金收據。請收好。

G：謝謝。

R：不客氣。祝您住店愉快。

Words and expressions（單詞和短語）

receptionist 接待員

check in 入住

of course 當然

deposit 押金

copy 副本

record 記錄

receipt 收據

Exercises（練習題）

1. Complete the sentences.（補全句子）

1. I'm afraid your room is not ready yet. Would you mind _____ for a while please? We're very sorry for the inconvenience.

您的房間恐怕還沒準備好，您介不介意稍等一會？抱歉使您不方便。

2. How much a day do you _____?

每天收費多少？

3. It is hundred yuan a day _____ heating fee, but excluding service charge.

一百元一天，包括供暖費但不包括服務費。

4. It's quite _____.

收費十分合理。

5. How long do you intend to _____ in this hotel?

您準備住多久？

6. Have you got through with the _____ procedure?

你是否已經辦妥住宿登記手續？

7. Can I book a single room for my friend beforehand as he will _____ in Shanghai tomorrow morning?

我能為我的朋友預訂一間單人房嗎？他將於明天早上到達上海。

8. Would you mind _____ in this form and pay a hundred yuan in advance for him.

請填好這個表，並預付一百元錢。

9. This is a receipt for paying in _____. Please keep it.

這是預付款收據，請收好。

10. Have you any _____ room in the hotel?

旅館裡有空餘房間嗎？

11. Sorry, we have no vacant (spare) room for you. But I can _____ you to the Orient Hotel where you may get a spare room.

對不起，我們已經客滿了。但是我可以介紹您去東方飯店，那裡有空餘的房間。

12. Good afternoon, my _____ number is 321. Any mail for me?

下午好！我的房號是321。有我的信嗎？

13. How would you like to settle your _____?

您打算如何付款？

14. You forgot to put in the date of your _____.

您忘了填寫離店日期了。

15. _____ much do I have to pay for you?

我要付多少錢？

16. Please sign at the _____ on the right hand side.

請在右下角簽名。

17. Yes, we _____ have a reservation for you.

對了，我們這兒是有您預訂的房間。

18. Would you please fill out this form while I prepare your _____ for you?

請您把這份表填好，我同時就給您製作房卡，好嗎？

19. What should I fill in under _____?

「房間號碼」這一欄我該怎麼填呢？

20. I'll put in the room number for you _____ on.

過會兒我來給您填上房間號碼。

21. But I'm afraid that it will be necessary for us to ask you to _____ rooms for the last two nights.

不過，恐怕最後兩天我們得請您搬到別的房間去。

22. And here is your _____, Mr. Bradley. Your room number is 1420.

給您房間的鑰匙，布拉德利先生。您的房間號碼是 1420。

23. It is on the 14th floor and the _____ rate is $ 90.

房間在 14 層，每天的房費是 90 美元。

24. Please make _____ that you have it with you all the time.

請務必隨時帶著它。

II. Make a dialogue according to the following situation. （創作情景對話）

已經預定的客人 B 來到前臺想辦理入住手續，前臺服務員 A 查完預定信息後，請對方出示護照或者身分證等有效證件，然後請客人填寫入住登記表，辦完登記入住後告訴客人房間號是 1008，請門童送客人到房間。請根據以上情景，創作一篇不少於 100 個單詞的英文對話。

Unit 3　Bell Service　應接服務

Background（背景知識）

Many tasks and responsibilities make up a bellman job description. Transporting guest luggage is one of the main bellman duties. At luxury hotels, bell service staff are typically responsible for unloading luggage at curbside upon a guest's arrival, as well as delivering the luggage to a guest's room after check-in. Bell service staff also store luggage for guests as needed before or after check-in/check-out, and usually load it directly into the taxicab or rental vehicle upon request.

Bell service at hotels also includes delivery of food and other items to a guest room. Some hotels offer 24-hour room service, so guests can have a cheeseburger, a bottle of wine or a new razor blade delivered to their door even in the wee hours of the night. Bellmen may also assist guests with laundry service.

Bellman responsibilities include assisting guests with making arrangements for local activities. They help guests buy tickets to shows or local attractions, make reservations at restaurants and arrange for a massage or spa treatment. Bellmen can also assist with getting a rental car, as well as calling for and to hail a cab for guests. Bell service staff often give advice on local things to do and see, recommending restaurants in various price ranges and local attractions.

Situational dialogues (情景對話)

Dialogue 1

B—Bellboy   G—Guest

B: Good afternoon, sir. Welcome to our hotel. I will show you to your room. You have two suitcases and one bag; is that right?

G: Yes, that's right.

B: Is there anything valuable or breakable in your bag?

G: Yes, there is a bottle of whiskey.

B: Could you carry this bag, sir? I'm afraid the contents may break.

G: Sure, no problem.

B: Thank you. This way, sir.

B: This is your room. May I have your key, sir? After you, sir. May I put your bags here?

G: Sure, just put them anywhere.

B: This room faces south. Are you satisfied with it, sir?

G: Yes, it's nice.

B: Thanks. By the way, you probably know that the tap water here is undrinkable. You can drink boiled water or bottled water.

G: Thank you for telling me.

B: If there is anything we can do for you, please let us know. The extension number for the front desk is 「6」.

G：OK, thanks.

Translation（譯文）

B——行李員　G——客人

B：下午好，先生。歡迎光臨本酒店。我將帶您去您的房間。您有兩個行李箱和一個包，對嗎？

G：是的，沒錯。

B：您的包裡有什麼貴重或易碎物品嗎？

G：是的，有一瓶威士忌。

B：先生，您能拿這個包嗎？我怕會打破裡面的東西。

G：當然，沒問題。

B：謝謝您！這邊請，先生。

B：這是您的房間。請把鑰匙給我一下，先生。您先請，先生。我可以把您的行李放在這裡嗎？

G：當然，放在哪裡都行。

B：這個房間朝南。您覺得滿意嗎，先生？

G：是的，很好。

B：謝謝。順便說一下，您可能知道，這裡的自來水是不能飲用的。您可以喝開水或瓶裝水。

G：謝謝您的提醒。

B：如果有什麼吩咐，請跟我們說。前臺的分機號碼是「6」。

G：好的，謝謝。

Words and expressions（單詞和短語）

bell service 禮賓服務

bellmen 行李員，服務生

suitcase 衣箱

valuable 貴重的

breakable 易碎的

bottle 瓶

whiskey 威士忌

content 內容

break 摔破

after you 您先請

be satisfied with 滿意

probably 很可能
tap water 自來水
undrinkable 不可飲用
boiled water 開水
bottled water 瓶裝水
extension number 分機號

Dialogue 2

B—Bellboy G—Guest

B：Here is your room, Mrs. Simpson. After you, please.

G：Thank you.

B：Shall I draw the curtains for you?

G：Yes, thank you. Oh, wonderful. My room just faces the little mountain. The flowers are in blossom.

B：I'm very happy you like it.

G：How can I make tea or coffee?

B：You can make your own tea and coffee using the electric kettle on the desk.

G：Is there a hair salon in your hotel?

B：Yes, it is on the left side of the south gate. It is open from 9 a.m. to 11 p.m.

G：Can you tell me something about the Chinese restaurant of your hotel?

B：Certainly. we are good at Beijing food. You can try Beijing roast duck here. By the way, it is the Mid-Autumn Festival today, one of the Chinese traditional festivals. You can try all kinds of moon cakes.

G：Thank you very much. It's my birthday today. I want to spend the Chinese birthday with my parents at the Chinese restaurant in the hotel.

B：Wonderful. The Chinese restaurant will present you with a bowl of longevity noodles with a poached egg.

G：Why?

B：In the eyes of Chinese people, noodles symbolize longevity, while poached egg will bring good luck to you.

G：It's very nice of you. Where is your service brochure? I want to get more information about the facilities and services of the hotel.

B：It's in the first drawer of the dresser. Is there anything else I can do for you?

G：No, nothing. Here's something for you.

B: It's very kind of you, but I'm afraid we don't accept it. Thank you all the same. If there's anything I can do for you, please call me. I'm always at your service. Happy birthday!

Translation（譯文）

B——行李員　G——客人

B：辛普森太太，這是您的房間。您先請。

G：謝謝你！

B：我為您拉上窗簾好嗎？

G：好的，謝謝你。哦，太棒了。我的房間就面對著小山。鮮花盛開。

B：您喜歡，我真高興。

G：我怎麼泡茶或者煮咖啡？

B：您可以用桌上的電熱壺自己泡茶和煮咖啡。

G：你們酒店有美髮廳嗎？

B：有的，在南門的左邊。營業時間是上午9點到晚上11點。

G：你能介紹一下你們酒店的中餐廳嗎？

B：當然可以。我們擅長做北京菜。您可以嘗嘗北京烤鴨。順便說一下，今天是中秋節，中國的傳統節日之一。您可以品嘗各種各樣的月餅。

G：非常感謝。今天是我的生日。我想和我的父母在酒店的中餐廳過中國生日。

B：太棒了。中餐廳將送您一碗長壽面和一個荷包蛋。

G：為什麼？

B：在中國人的觀念裡，麵條是長壽的象徵，而荷包蛋將給您帶來好運。

G：你太好了。服務手冊在哪裡？我想瞭解更多關於酒店的設施和服務的信息。

B：在梳妝臺第一個抽屜裡。還有什麼我可以幫忙的嗎？

G：沒有了。這是給你的。

B：您真好，不過我恐怕不能接受，但還是要感謝您。如果有什麼我可以幫您，請給我打電話。我隨時為您效勞。生日快樂！

Words and expressions（單詞和短語）

curtain 窗簾

in bloom 開花

electric kettle 電水壺

hair salon 美髮廳

roast duck 烤鴨

Mid-Autumn Festival 中秋節

traditional 傳統的

moon cake 月餅

all kinds of 各種各樣的

spend 花費

birthday 生日

parent 父母

present 送給

longevity 長壽

noodle 麵條

poached egg 荷包蛋

symbolize 象徵

luck 運氣

brochure 小冊子

information 信息

facility 設施

accept 接受

Dialogue 3

A—Concierge　B—Guest

A：How are you, Mr. Lowrance?

B：Fine, thank you very much. And you?

A：I'm good, thanks. May I help you?

B：Ah, yes. You know, tomorrow is the Valentine's Day. I am thinking about a surprise for my wife. Any idea?

A：How about flowers? A bunch of flowers on the Valentine's Day would be very romantic.

B：Haha, old tricks. But they always work, right? So where shall I get the flowers? Are there any flower shops nearby?

A：You can leave it to me, if you don't mind. The hotel also provides superior flower service. The roses on the Valentine's Day are specially transported from Bulgaria by air.

B：Very well. 99 red roses will be enough. Oh, she loves lily. Make them 10.

A：Alright, Mr. Gordon. 99 roses plus 10 lilies. Would you like to leave a couple of words to her? Here is the card.

B：Lovely. Here you go. That's perfect.

A：Shall I send the flowers to your room, Mr. Lowrance?

B：Yes, around nine on tomorrow morning.

A：Very well.

B: And would you mind reserving two street-view seats at the Chinese restaurant? I heard the steaks there are supreme.

A: Not at all, sir.

Translation（譯文）

A——禮賓員　B——客人

A：洛倫斯先生，您好嗎？

B：很好，非常感謝。你呢？

A：我很好，謝謝。有什麼需要幫忙嗎？

B：啊，是的。你知道，明天是情人節。我想給我太太一個驚喜。你有什麼點子嗎？

A：送花怎麼樣？情人節送一束花會很浪漫。

B：哈哈，太老套了。但是一直很管用，對吧？那麼，該去哪裡買花呢？附近有花店嗎？

A：如果您不介意的話，可以交給我去辦。酒店還提供優越的鮮花服務。情人節的玫瑰是從保加利亞空運過來的。

B：很好。99朵紅玫瑰應該夠了。哦，她喜歡百合。要10朵百合吧。

A：好了，戈登先生。99朵玫瑰加10朵百合花。您想給她送幾句話嗎？這是卡片。

B：很好。給你。太完美了。

A：我需要送花到您的房間嗎，洛倫斯先生？

B：是的，明天早上，大約9點。

A：很好。

B：還有，您介意在中餐館幫我預訂兩個街景餐位嗎？我聽說那裡的牛排是頂級的。

A：沒問題，先生。

Words and expressions（單詞和短語）

the Valentine's Day 情人節

surprise 驚喜

bunch 束

romantic 浪漫的

trick 惡作劇

work 有效

nearby 在附近

superior 優良的

transport 運輸

Bulgaria 保加利亞

by air 空運

lily 百合花

a couple of 一對，幾個

perfect 完美的

steak 牛排

supreme 最高的

Exercises（練習題）

I. Complete the sentences.（補全句子）

1. May I help you _____ your bags?
讓我幫您提行李好嗎？

2. Let me take the _____ for you. I'll show you to the Front Desk. This way, please.
讓我幫您搬行李吧。我們去前臺報到，請這邊走。

3. I'll check with my _____ for that.
這事我得請示主管。

4. That's very kind of you, but I'm afraid we don't accept _____. Thank you all the same.
您真是太好了，不過我們是不收小費的。還是一樣要謝謝您。

5. If there is anything I can do for you, please _____.
如果有什麼我能效勞的，請給我打電話。

6. All the rooms in our hotel are quite large, and the rooms on this side of the building have a lovely _____.
我們飯店房間都相當大的，樓這一側的房間外的景色都很棒。

7. May I have your _____, please?
請把取物牌給我好嗎？

8. I'm the _____ who brings you the luggage, sir.
先生，我是酒店的服務員，替您拿行李的。

9. Today is a rainy day and the floor is _____ so please be careful.
今天下雨，地面濕滑，請小心走。

10. Could you make sure that your bags are _____ before you leave?
請您在離開前確認行李打包好了嗎？

11. Here's the _____ and there's the bathroom.
這兒是壁櫥。這兒是洗澡間。

12. Is there anything _____, sir?
還有什麼事嗎，先生？

13. Here's the light _____.
这是电灯开关。

14. Let me help you _____ your luggage.
我来帮您拿行李。

15. It's very _____ of you to do so.
你这样做使我很感激。

16. What's your room _____, please?
请问您的房间号码?

17. And _____, could I have a look at your room card?
顺便问一句, 我可以看一下您的房卡吗?

18. How do you _____ this room?
您觉得这个房间怎么样?

19. It's also quite _____.
房间也很宽敞。

20. Do you mind if I put your luggage by the _____?
我把您的行李搁在衣柜旁边好吗?

21. By the way, could you tell me _____ your hotel service?
顺便问问, 你能不能给我讲一下宾馆服务的情况?

22. Is there any place in the hotel where we can _____ ourselves?
旅馆里有娱乐场所吗?

23. If you want to take a _____, you can go to the garden.
如果您想散步, 可以去花园。

24. There is a _____ centre on the ground floor.
在一楼有个娱乐中心。

25. You can play billiards, table tennis, bridge, and go _____.
您可以去打打台球、乒乓球、桥牌和保龄球。

26. Is there a place where we can listen to some _____?
有听音乐的地方吗?

27. And where can I have my _____ done?
脏衣服送到哪里去洗?

28. Would you please tell me the _____ service hours of the dining room?
请告诉我餐厅每天的服务时间, 好吗?

29. From 7: 00 a.m. till 10: 00 p.m. nearly serving all day _____.
从早上七时一直到晚上十时, 几乎全天供应。

30. When will the bar and cafe _____?

酒吧和咖啡館什麼時間開放？

II. Make a dialogue according to the following situation. （創作情景對話）

禮賓員 C 帶客人 B 從前天右邊的電梯去房間，給客人介紹酒店內的服務設施和地點，如商務中心，西餐廳，ATM，健身房等以及酒店周邊的公交線路。最後如有什麼需要可以到禮賓部來諮詢。請根據以上情景，創作一篇不少於 100 個單詞的英文對話。

Unit 4　Telephone Operator　總機服務

Background（背景知識）

Most of hotels have their own switchboard（總機）. And the duties and responsibilities of the hotel telephone operator are as follows：

Speaks clearly, distinctly, and with a friendly, courteous tone.

Uses listening skills to put callers at ease and obtains accurate, complete information.

Answers incoming calls and directs them to guest rooms through the telephone console or to hotel personnel or departments.

Takes and distributes messages for guests.

Provides information on guest services, and answers inquires about public hotel events.

Situational dialogues（情景對話）

Dialogue 1

G—Guest　O—Operator

O：Operator. May I help you?

G：Well, I'd like to place a call to a friend in the US.

O：Alright, sir. Is this a paid call or collect call?

G：Paid call, please.

O：Person-to-person or station-to-station, sir?

G：Person-to-person.

O：Could you tell me the party's full name and telephone number, please?

G：Yes, it's Stephen Louis and the number is New York 982-1675.

O：Mr. Stephen Louis at New York 982-1675.

G：That's correct.

O: May I have your name and room number, please?

G: Yes, it's James Phillis in Room 1666.

O: Mr. James Phillis in Room 1666.

G: That's right.

O: Could you please hang up now? We will contact New York and then call you back.

G: Sure, thanks.

(After a while)

O: May I speak to Mr. Phillis?

G: Yes. This is Phillis Speaking.

O: This is the Hotel Operator. Mr. Louis from New York is on the line. Go ahead, please.

G: Thanks a lot.

Translation（譯文）

O——接線員　G——客人

O：接線員。請問需要幫助嗎？

G：嗯，我想打電話給一位美國的朋友。

O：好的，先生。您需要本方付費電話還是對方付費電話？

G：本方付費電話。

O：叫人還是叫號電話，先生？

G：叫人。

O：您能告訴我對方的全名和電話號碼嗎？

G：好的，斯蒂芬·路易斯，紐約的號碼是 982-1675。

O：斯蒂芬·路易斯先生，紐約 982-1675。

G：對。

O：請告訴我您的名字和房號，可以嗎？

G：好的，我是 1666 房間的詹姆斯·菲利斯。

O：1666 房間的詹姆斯·菲利斯先生。

G：沒錯。

O：您先把電話掛了好嗎？我們先聯繫紐約，然後給您回電話。

G：當然，謝謝。

(過了一會兒)

O：我可以和菲利斯先生通話嗎？

G：可以的。我是菲利斯。

O：這是酒店接線員。紐約的路易斯先生正在線上。請開始通話吧。

G：非常感謝。

Chapter One Front Office 前廳部

Words and expressions（單詞和短語）

switchboard 總機

operator 接線員

place a call 撥打電話

paid call 本方付費電話

collect call 對方付費電話

person-to-person 叫人

station-to-station 叫號

full name 全名

correct 正確的

hang up 掛斷

contact 聯繫

on the line 在線的

go ahead 開始，繼續

Dialogue 2

G—Guest   O—Operator

G：Operator. I wonder if your hotel has morning call service.

O：Yes. Anyone who stays in our hotel can ask for the service. Would you like a morning call?

G：Yes. I'd like to be woken up at 6：30 tomorrow morning.

O：What kind of call would you like? By phone or by knocking at the door?

G：By phone, please. I don't want to disturb my neighbors.

O：Sure. Let me confirm your name and room number.

G：Anna Chen in room 345.

O：Mrs. Chen in room 345, tomorrow morning at 6：30. OK, we will give you a call in the morning. Anything else I can do for you?

G：No. Thank you.

O：You are welcome, madam. Have a sound sleep.

Translation（譯文）

O——接線員   G——客人

G：你好，接線員。請問你們酒店是否有叫早服務呢？

O：有的。我們酒店的住客可以要求這項服務。您需要叫早嗎？

G：是的。我希望明天早上六點半起床。

O：您想要什麼樣的叫醒方式，打電話或敲門？
G：請打電話吧。我不想打擾隔壁客人。
O：沒問題。我想確認一下您的姓名和房號。
G：安娜·陳，345房間。
O：345房間的陳太太，明天早上六點半。好的，我們將在早上給您電話。還有什麼可以幫忙的嗎？
G：沒有了。謝謝你。
O：不客氣，夫人。祝您晚安。

Words and expressions（單詞和短語）

wonder 想知道

morning call 叫醒服務

wake up 叫醒

knock at the door 敲門

disturb 打擾

neighbor 鄰居

confirm 確認

sound sleep 酣睡

Dialogue 3

O—Operator   G—Guest

O: This is the Hotel Operator. May I help you?

G: Yes, I'd like to make an overseas call.

O: You may call direct from your room, sir. It is cheaper than booking it through the operator.

G: Oh, I didn't know that.

O: The country codes are listed in the Service Directory in your room. Please dial 001 before the country code and number. Please do not dial 0 before the entire number as you would do for an outside call.

G: I see. 001 and then country code, area code and number.

O: That's right, sir.

G: By the way, what is the charge for an overseas call?

O: That will be $2.3 per minute.

G: Can I pay by my account?

O: Certainly. Calls are automatically charged to your account.

G：Thank you very much.

O：You're always welcome, sir.

Translation（譯文）

O——接線員　G——客人

O：這裡是酒店接線員。請問有什麼需要幫忙嗎？

G：是的，我想打國際長途電話。

O：您可以直接從房間撥打，先生。它比通過接線員要便宜。

G：哦，這點我不知道。

O：您房間服務目錄裡列出了各國的代碼。請您在國家代碼和電話號碼前撥001。整個號碼前請不要撥0。那是您打外線電話才需要的。

G：明白了。001，然後是國家代碼，區號和電話號碼。

O：是的，先生。

G：順便問一下，國際長途電話怎麼收費？

O：每分鐘2.3美元。

G：我可以用我的帳戶支付嗎？

O：當然。話費將自動記到您的帳戶。

G：非常感謝。

O：請別客氣，先生。

Words and expressions（單詞和短語）

overseas 海外的

direct 直接的

cheap 便宜的

country 國家

code 代號

service directory 服務目錄

dial 撥號

entire 全部的

outside call 外線電話

charge 費用，收費

account 帳戶

automatically 自動地

Dialogue 4

O—Operator　G—Guest

G: Is this Beijing Hotel?

O: Speaking (Yes, it is). May I help you?

G: Yes. Could you put me through to Room 213, please?

O: Certainly, sir. Just a moment, please … I'm sorry, the line is busy. Would you like to hold on or call back later.

G: It's OK. I will call back later. Thank you.

O: You're welcome, sir.

Translation（譯文）

O——接線員　G——客人

G：請問是北京飯店嗎？

O：正是。請問有什麼可以幫您嗎？

G：是的。請幫我接通213房間，好嗎？

O：當然可以，先生。請稍等……對不起，線路正忙。您想繼續等待還是過後再打過來呢？

G：沒事。我待會再打過來。謝謝你！

O：不用客氣，先生。

Words and expressions（單詞和短語）

hold on 別掛電話

put through 接通

Exercises（練習題）

I. Complete the sentences.（補全句子）

1. International Hotel. May I _____ you?
國際大酒店，我可以幫您嗎？

2. I'm putting you through, sir. I'm sorry, there's no _____. Would you like to leave a message or to call back?
我給您接過去，先生。對不起，沒有人聽電話，您是留言還是再打過來？

3. Hold on, please. I'll put you _____ to the information?
請別掛，我幫您轉到前臺問詢。

4. I'm sorry, sir. But the manager's line is _____. I'll call you back when it is free.
對不起，先生。經理電話占線，線路通時我給您打過來。

5. This is the _____. May I help you?
這是總機，我可以幫您嗎？

6. We have a computer wake-up service, please _____ 5 first and then the wake-up

time.

我們有電腦叫醒服務，請先撥 5，然後撥叫醒時間。

7. Our computer will _____ the time and your room number.

電腦將記錄下您的叫醒時間和房號。

8. Excuse me for asking but which _____ are you calling?

對不起，請問您要往哪個國家打電話？

9. Which city, please? Do you know the city area _____?

請問時哪個城市？您知道區號嗎？

10. Could you _____ the number, please?

請您重複一下電話號碼，好嗎？

11. Would you like a pay call or a _____ call, madam?

女士，您是要撥直接付款電話還是要對方付款電話？

12. May I _____ you there is still a handling charge?

我還要提醒您一下，另外還有手續費。

13. I'll connect you to Mr. Smith's room _____ away.

我馬上為您接 Smith 先生房間。

14. Please _____ the line a moment. I'm putting you through to his office.

請不要放電話，我這就給您接待他辦公室去。

15. You're _____, sir.

先生，給您接通了。

16. I'm afraid all calls to abroad must go through the _____.

抱歉，恐怕所有的國籍長途電話都要通過接線員。

17. By phone. I don't want to _____ my neighbors.

電話叫醒，我不想吵醒鄰居。

18. Would you like to leave a _____?

您要留言嗎？

19. The country codes are listed in the Services _____ in your room.

國家代號列在您房間裡的服務指南上。

20. I'm afraid there's no _____ from Room 325.

325 房恐怕沒人接電話。

21. Your call to Los Angeles lasted 10 minutes. It will _____ 10 U. S. dollars. We'll add it to your final room bill.

您打到洛杉磯的電話持續了十分鐘，費用十美元，我們將一併加算在最終的宿費帳單上。

22. It's a _____ call.

這是接聽人付費的電話。

23. So I would _____ to request an early morning call.

因此我想讓你們明天早上叫醒我。

24. But I have to be at the _____ room of the Garden Hotel in Tianjin by 10 o'clock.

但我是10點鐘必須趕到天津花園賓館會議室。

25. That means that I'll have to be on the road _____ 7 o'clock at the latest.

就是說我明天早晨最遲也要7點鐘上路。

26. In that _____, I would like you to call me at 5：45?

那樣的話,你們明早5點45分叫醒我好嗎?

27. OK. So we will _____ you up at 5：45 tomorrow morning.

好,那麼我們明早5點45分叫醒您。

28. Will you do me a _____, Miss?

小姐,能幫個忙嗎?

29. I _____ if your hotel has the morning call service.

不知道你們飯店是否有叫早服務。

II. *Make a dialogue according to the following situation.* （創作情景對話）

客人B是一位來自美國的客人,他想打國際長途回美國的家裡,打電話到總機,總機服務員告訴客人B,從酒店打國際長途的話,要先按0,然後再撥國家代號,美國州的代號,最後撥打家裡電話。請根據以上情景,創作一篇不少於100個單詞的英文對話。

Unit 5　Business Center　商務中心

Background（背景知識）

The Business Centers in high level star-rate hotels provide comprehensive office facilities and services, including PC rental（個人電腦出租）, broadband service（寬帶服務）, fax, photocopying, conference services, professional secretarial services（專業秘書服務）, international communication facilities（國際通訊設備）, booking tickets etc.

Passenger train, express train, motor train, high speed rail, round-trip ticket, one-way ticket, arrival time, lower (middle, upper) birth, hard seat, soft seat, business class, second class, economy class, television, computer, video recorder, sound recorder, projector, microphone, speaker, white board, Internet, simultaneous interpretation system, small-sized, middle-sized, large-sized, conference room, meeting hall, multifunctional hall, exhibition center, banquet hall, waiting room, decoration, ornamentation, banquet hall, typing, photocopy, fax, scan

Situational dialogues（情景對話）

Dialogue 1

A——Clerk　B——Guest

A：Good morning, Mr. Clayton. Is there anything I can do for you?

B：Yes. I'd like to ask you to send an express mail for me.

A：What is it?

B：It's a document of my company.

A：What way of delivery do you prefer?

B：What ways do you have?

A：There are two ways, express delivery and ordinary.

B：Express delivery, please.

A：The charge is 12 yuan for your express mail.

B：No problem.

A：Could you please fill in this express mail application form? May I have your telephone number?

B：139-7954-1824.

A：What's your room number, please?

B：3206.

A：Show me your room card, please?

B：Here you are.

A：Thank you. This is your bill. Do you pay now or add it to your room charge?

B：Add it to my room charge.

A：Alright. I would notify the express mail service to fetch it immediately.

B：Thank you. Good bye.

A：Good bye. Have a nice stay.

Translation（譯文）

A——職員　B——客人

A：早上好，克萊頓先生。有什麼可以幫忙的嗎?

B：是的。我想請你幫我寄一個快件。

A：是什麼物品呢?

B：是我公司的一份文檔。

A：您喜歡哪種寄件方式？

B：你們有哪些？

A：有兩種方式，特快和普通。

B：請用特快吧。

A：特快的費用是 12 元。

B：沒問題。

A：能請您填寫這份快件申請表嗎？請提供一下您的電話號碼，好嗎？

B：139-7954-1824。

A：請問您的房號是？

B：3206。

A：請出示您的房卡好嗎？

B：給你。

A：謝謝您！這是您的帳單。您付現金還是記到您的房費？

B：記到房費吧。

A：好的。我馬上通知特快專遞來取件。

B：謝謝你！再見。

A：再見。祝您住店愉快。

Words and expressions（單詞和短語）

business center 商務中心

express 快速

document 文件

company 公司

delivery 投遞

prefer 更喜歡

ordinary 普通的

charge 費用

application 申請

bill 帳單

cash 現金

fetch 去取

Dialogue 2

C—Clerk　G—Guest

C: Good morning, sir. Can I help you?

G: I'm going to have a congress tomorrow. I'd like to book some facilities and personnel for it.

C: No problem, sir. Here is the rate list.

G: Thank you.

C: My pleasure. Tomorrow, that's June 12th, isn't it?

G: Yes, I need an auditorium for 40 people, a projector and a video-camera.

C: 40 people… I suggest you to rent a small auditorium; that'll be enough.

G: Good idea. I also need an interpreter and two messengers.

C: I see. Could you please sign here? And fill in your telephone number, please.

G: OK.

C: Thank you, sir. Everything will be ready at 9:00 a.m. tomorrow. Could you come and check it?

G: Sure. Thanks.

C: You're welcome, sir. We look forward to serving you.

Translation（譯文）

C—職員　G—客人

C：早上好，先生。需要幫忙嗎？

G：明天我有個會議。我想預訂一些設施和工作人員。

C：沒問題，先生。這是價目表。

G：謝謝你。

C：不客氣。明天，也就是6月12日，對嗎？

G：是的。我需要一個40人的禮堂、一個投影儀和一個攝像機。

C：40人……我建議您租一間小禮堂就行了。

G：好主意。我還需要一個口譯員和兩個信息員。

C：我明白了。您在這裡簽個名好嗎？還有，請留下您的電話號碼。

G：好的。

C：謝謝您，先生。明天上午9點，一切都會準備就緒。您能來檢查一下嗎？

G：當然。謝謝。

C：不客氣，先生。我們期待著為您服務。

Words and expressions（單詞和短語）

clerk 辦事員

congress 國會，會議

facility 設施

personnel 人員

rate list 價目表

auditorium 禮堂

projector 投影儀

suggest 建議

video-camera 攝像機

rent 租用

interpreter 口譯員

messenger 信息員

look forward to 期盼

Dialogue 3

C—Clerk　G—Guest

C: Good morning, Mr. Cornell. Is there anything I can do for you?

G: I want to rent a notebook computer.

C: For how long?

G: One night only. I will send it back tomorrow morning.

C: There are several brands of computers in the center, such as Lenovo, HP, IBM and Toshiba. What brand do you prefer?

G: IBM.

C: Please fill in this form. This is the hotel management regulation related to facilities rented out. Please read the details careful.

G: What about the charges?

C: The charge is ¥10 per hour. You need to pay 2,000 yuan as a deposit in advance.

G: OK.

C: Could you please show me your room card?

G: Sure. How about the configuration of the computer?

C: It is a new one. The configuration is good and the random access memory is large enough.

G: Does the Internet run fast enough in my room?

C: All rooms in our hotel are equipped with broadband connection. The Internet runs very fast.

G: Wonderful. I'm a person of impatience. I feel anxious when the net speed is slow.

C: So am I. If you type something in the computer, please don't forget to keep a copy, because our technician will format the hard disk after it is returned.

G：You're so kind. See you.

C：Bye. Have a nice day.

Translation（譯文）

C——職員　G——客人

C：早上好，康奈爾先生。有什麼我可以幫忙的嗎？

G：我想租一臺筆記本電腦。

C：租多長時間？

G：只要一個晚上。明天早上我會歸還。

C：商務中心有幾個品牌的電腦，如聯想、惠普、IBM 和東芝。您喜歡什麼牌子的？

G：IBM。

C：請填寫這張表格。這是酒店設施出租物品管理相關規定。請仔細閱讀。

G：租金是多少呢？

C：每小時 10 元。您需要預付 2,000 元作為押金。

G：好的。

C：請您出示一下房卡好嗎？

G：當然。電腦的配置怎麼樣？

C：這是一臺新的機子。配置好，隨機存取內存足夠大。

G：我的房間網路速度夠快嗎？

C：我們賓館所有房間都配備了寬帶。網速非常快。

G：太棒了。我是一個急性子。如果網速慢，我會焦慮。

C：我也是。如果您在電腦裡輸入信息，請別忘了保留備份，因為我們的技術人員將在電腦歸還後格式化硬盤。

G：您真好。回頭見。

C：再見。祝您住店愉快。

Words and expressions（單詞和短語）

notebook computer 筆記本電腦

brand 品牌

fill in 填寫

management 管理

regulation 規定

related to 與……有關的

detail 細節

deposit 押金

in advance 預先

configuration 配置

random access memory 內存

be equipped with 配備

broadband 寬帶

impatience 不耐煩

anxious 焦急的

type 打字

technician 技術員

format 格式化

hard disk 硬盤

Dialogue 4

C—Clerk   G—Guest

C: Good morning, Mr. Bellamy. How can I help you?

G: I would like to have these materials typed. Can you help me?

C: Sure. When do you need it?

G: Before this evening. Is that OK?

C: Yes. Do you have any special requirements, such as the size of paper, font or margin?

G: Oh, yes. Please use A4 paper. Times New Roman for the title and Arial for the text.

C: And the size of the font?

G: The title should be 14 and the text 11.

C: Very well, sir. Shall I send it to your room after I finish typing?

G: Eh, no. Send it to the café. I'll be there after dinner. By the way, how do you charge?

C: It's 6 yuan per page.

G: That's not cheap. Alright, I'll leave it to you.

C: One more thing, Mr. Bellamy. Shall I staple the documents by then?

G: Yes, please. It's very considerate of you.

Translation（譯文）

C——職員   G——客人

C：貝拉米先生，早上好。您需要幫忙嗎？

G：我想找人打出這些材料。你能幫我嗎？

C：當然可以。您什麼時候需要？

G：今晚之前。可以嗎？

C：可以的。您有什麼特殊要求，比如紙張的大小，字體或者頁邊距？

G：哦，有的。請使用 A4 紙。標題用 Times New Roman 字體，正文用 Arial。
C：字體的大小呢？
G：標題應該是 14 號，正文 11 號。
C：很好，先生。我打完字後需要送到您的房間嗎？
G：嗯，沒有。把它送到咖啡館。晚飯後，我會在那裡。順便問一下，你們怎麼收費？
C：每頁 6 元。
G：這有點貴。好吧，我把它交給你辦理。
C：還有一件事，貝拉米先生。屆時需要我裝訂文檔嗎？
G：要的，麻煩你了。你真是服務周到。

Words and expressions（單詞和短語）

material 材料

requirement 必要的條件

font 字體

margin 頁邊的空白

title 標題

café 咖啡館

one more thing 還有一件事

staple 把……訂起來

considerate 考慮周到的

Exercises（練習題）

I. Complete the sentences.（補全句子）

1. Excuse me, Sir, here is _____ area.
對不起先生，這裡是非抽菸區。

2. Would you like some _____?
請問您要喝點水嗎？

3. How many _____ would you like?
您需要複印多少份？

4. Would you like to make it a little _____?
要不要我（把顏色）調淺一些？

5. Here is your _____ file.
這是您的原件。

6. I'll leave the original file here. Please call me when the copy is _____.
我把原件先放在這裡，等複印好了就打電話通知我吧。

7. Would you like me to _____ these for you?
我為您裝訂好這些好嗎?

8. Shall I staple them on the left side or at the _____?
我是裝訂在左側還是上邊呢?

9. Shall I _____ this to fit A4 paper?
我是不是把它放大到適合 A4 的紙張呢?

10. Shall I copy these on both _____ of the paper?
我進行雙面複印好嗎?

11. The paper is _____.
卡紙了。

12. It is out of _____.
沒墨了。

13. Your original is not very clear. I can't _____ the copy will be good.
您的原件不太清晰,我不能保證複印件的效果很好。

14. I'd like to send a _____.
我想要發份傳真。

15. It's 10 yuan per minute for a fax to Beijing, including/excluding _____ charge.
發傳真到北京是每分鐘 10 元,包括/不包括服務費。

16. The _____ charge is 15 Yuan.
最低收費是 15 元。

17. Please write down the area _____ and the number.
請寫下區號和對方的號碼。

18. The paper is too _____. It may jam the machine.
這張紙太厚,可能會卡紙的。

19. Shall I make a _____ of this, and then send the copy?
我複印一份,然後將複印件傳真過去好嗎?

20. We have _____ a fax for you should we send it to your room or collect it by yourself?
我們收到給您的一份傳真。我們把它送上您的房間還是您自己下來取?

21. What _____ and size would you like?
您想要什麼字體,多大號的?

22. Could you _____ it?
您檢查一下好嗎?

23. How _____ does it take for a letter to go to America from Beijing?

信從北京到美國要多久？

24. Would you want the Image _____?
請問您要掃描嗎？

25. What format would you like to _____?
請問您要想以什麼格式儲存掃描的文件呢？

26. How would you like to pay? Charge to your room or by _____?
請問您的付款方式是什麼？轉房帳還是付現金呢？

27. May I have your _____ card please?
我可以看一下您的邀請卡嗎？

28. Here is the _____ of 8 Yuan for you.
這是找您的 8 元錢。

29. Please check the _____ scan before you place information on the memory stick or disk.
您使用 U 盤或磁盤時，請先執行掃描病毒後再使用。

II. Make a dialogue according to the following situation.（創作情景對話）

客人 B 來到商務中心發傳真。服務員 D 告訴客人收費標準。然後服務員按照發傳真的程序將傳真文件正文朝下，放入紙槽內，撥國家代號或者地區區號，傳真號碼，聽到對方傳真信號後，按啓動鍵。請根據以上情景，創作一篇不少於 100 個單詞的英文對話。

Unit 6　Complaints　處理投訴

Background（背景知識）

Front office management and staff should keep the following resolution guidelines in mind when handling guest complaints.

When expressing a complaint, the guest may be quite angry. Front office staff members should not make promises that exceed their authority.

Honesty is the best policy when dealing with guest complaints. If a problem cannot be solved, front office staff should admit this to the guest early on.

Front office staff should be advised that some guests complain as part of their nature. The staff should develop an approach for dealing with such guests.

Top 10 ways of handling guest complaints：

1. Listen with concern and empathy.

2. Isolate the guest if possible, so that other guests won't overhear.

3. Stay calm. Don't argue with the guest.

4. Be aware of the guest's self-esteem. Show a personal interest in the problem. Try to use the guest name frequently.

5. Give the guest your undivided attention. Concentrate on the problem, not on placing blame. Do not insult the guest.

6. Take notes. Writing down the key facts saves time if someone else must get involved. Also, the guests tend to slow down when they see the front desk agent trying to write down the issue.

7. Tell the guest what can be the best done. Offer choices. Don't promise the impossible, and don't exceed your authority.

8. Set an approximate time for completion of corrective actions. Be specific, but do not underestimate the amount of time it will take to resolve the problem.

9. Monitor the progress of the corrective action.

10. Follow up. Even if the complaint was resolved by someone else, contact the guest to ensure that the problem was resolved satisfactorily.

Situational dialogues（情景對話）

Dialogue 1

K—Guest   M—Manager

(Janet Kim checked into her room 15 minutes ago. She was surprised to find that the room is in such a mess. She asks to see the manager.)

M: What's the trouble, Madam?

K: I ask for hotel accommodation, not a cowshed. I've never seen anything more disgusting.

M: Hasn't the room been cleaned yet?

K: Of course not. The bathroom is in a total mess. There is no soap, no towels, not even toilet paper.

M: I'm extremely sorry to hear that. We do apologize for the inconvenience. I'll look into the matter and be back in a minute.

(After a while)

M: Well, Madam, there seems to have been a communication break-down between the front office and the housekeeping department. They have promised to give you a room that is fully up to standard.

K: The sooner, the better.

M: They'll be there in a minute. Sorry about the trouble.

Translation（譯文）

K——客人　M——經理

（珍妮・金 15 分鐘前住進她的房間。她驚訝地發現房間裡一團糟。她要求見經理。）

M：發生什麼事情了，夫人？

K：我需要的是酒店，而不是一個牛棚。我從沒見過比這更噁心的酒店了。

M：房間沒有打掃乾淨嗎？

K：當然沒有。浴室是一團糟。沒有肥皂、毛巾，甚至手紙。

M：聽到這個情況，我非常抱歉。我們為給您帶來的不便表示歉意。我會調查此事，很快就回來。

（過了一會兒）

M：夫人，前廳和客房服務部門好像有點溝通問題。他們已經承諾給您安排一個完全達到標準的房間。

K：越快越好。

M：他們很快就到位。再次抱歉。

Words and expressions（單詞和短語）

dealing with complaints 處理投訴

mess 混亂

manager 經理

trouble 麻煩

madam 夫人；女士

accommodation 住宿

cowshed 牛棚

disgusting 令人噁心的

bathroom 浴室

soap 肥皂

towel 毛巾

toilet paper 廁紙

extremely 極其

apologize 道歉

inconvenience 不方便

look into 調查

front office 前廳

housekeeping department 客房部

promise 允諾
standard 標準
communication 溝通
break-down 中斷

Dialogue 2

G—Guest   R—Receptionist

G: Good morning. I have a reservation for a single room. My name is Jeremy Lowell.

R: I'm sorry, sir. But we have already rented the room to someone else. And the hotel is all booked now.

G: Wait a minute. I made my reservation with this hotel two months ago. And now you tell me that I don't have a room here. You can't treat me like this. I'm an old customer of this hotel. Look, here is your confirmation letter.

R: I know. But if you had read our confirmation letter carefully you would have realized that we only have rooms for guests until 6:00 p.m. on the expected arrival date. We have no choice but to release the rooms if the guest fails to arrive before that time. You see it's already 9 o'clock now.

G: You know, I would have loved to check in before 6 o'clock more than anybody else. But the fact is that my flight has been delayed for three hours owing to bad weather.

R: I'm very sorry. But we do have no spare room. At this point, I can only try and see if I can get a room in a nearby hotel. We will arrange the transfer for you.

G: Well, that's the least you can do. I have to sleep somewhere.

R: Please take a seat and wait over there. I'll soon have something worked out for you.

Translation（譯文）

G——客人   R——接待員

G：早上好。我預訂了一間房。我的名字是杰里米·洛維。

R：對不起，先生。但是我們已經把那個房間租給別人了。現在酒店都訂滿了。

G：等一下。我兩個月前就預訂了。現在你告訴我，我在這裡沒有房間住了。你們不能這樣對待我。我是這個酒店的老客戶。看吧，這是你們的確認信。

R：我知道。但是如果您已經仔細閱讀過我們的確認信，就會明白，我們只為客人保留房間到預抵日期的下午6點。如果客人沒能在那個時間之前到達，我們別無選擇，只能取消房間預訂。您知道現在已經9點了。

G：你知道的，我比誰都希望6點之前入住。但事實是，我的航班由於惡劣天氣影響而延誤了三個小時。

R：我很抱歉。但是我們確實沒有多餘的房間。現在我只能試著看能否在附近的一家酒店找到一個房間。我們會安排送您過去。

G：嗯，這是你起碼可以做到的。我必須有地方睡覺。

R：請在那邊坐下，稍等一下。我會很快為您找到解決的辦法。

Words and expressions（單詞和短語）

treat 對待

customer 顧客

confirmation letter 確認信

realize 認識到

expect 預期

arrival date 到店日期

choice 選擇

release 釋放

fail 做不到

delay 耽誤

owe to 由於

spare 空餘的

arrange 安排

transfer 轉運

least 最少

work out 想辦法

Dialogue 3

G—Guest　R—Receptionist

G：(Angrily) Housekeeping? I want to speak to the manager now!

R：Is there anything wrong, sir?

G：My laundry. It is badly washed. Your service is terrible!

R：Our manager will be up in a minute, sir.

(Later)

M：Mr. Jackson, I'm the housekeeping manager, Dennis. Is there anything I can do for you?

G：Please take a look at these clothes! There is a hole on this shirt when it came back. The sweater shrank badly even though your room attendant has guaranteed that they will be carefully washed.

M: I'm terribly sorry for the mistake. We will pay for the damage. Could you buy a new one and give us the receipt? We will refund it.

G: They are my birthday presents! They're irreplaceable.

M: I'm sorry to hear that. Please accept my apology on behalf of the hotel. Could you please let us compensate for the cost?

G: I'll buy a new one when I go back home. I'll send you the receipt then!

M: We'll send you a bank draft as soon as possible, sir. Please accept our apology again.

Translation（譯文）

G——客人　R——接待員　M——經理

G：（憤怒地）是客房部嗎？現在我想跟經理說話！

R：出什麼事了，先生？

G：我的衣服被洗壞了。你們的服務真是太糟糕了！

R：先生，我們的經理一會兒就上去。

（稍後）

M：杰克遜先生，我是丹尼斯，客房部經理。有什麼我可以幫忙的嗎？

G：請看看這些衣服！送回來的時候這件襯衫上有一個洞。毛衣也嚴重縮水，雖然你的客戶服務員保證過會小心洗滌。

M：我為這個錯誤感到非常抱歉。我們將賠償損失。您可以買一件新的，然後給我們收據嗎？我們將賠償。

G：它們是我的生日禮物，是不可替代的！

M：我很抱歉聽到這個消息。請接受我代表酒店向您道歉。能否讓我們賠償成本呢？

G：我回家後買個新的。我給你寄收據！

M：我們會盡快寄給您一張銀行匯票，先生。請再次接受我們的道歉。

Words and expressions（單詞和短語）

angrily 生氣地

laundry 洗滌的衣物

shirt 襯衫

hole 洞

sweater 毛衣

shrink 縮水

room attendant 服務員

guarantee 保證

mistake 錯誤

damage 損壞

receipt 收據

refund 退款

irreplaceable 不能替代的

accept 接受

apology 道歉

on behalf of 代表

compensate 賠償

cost 成本

bank draft 銀行匯票

Exercises（練習題）

I. Complete the sentences.（補全句子）

1. Can you change the room for me? It's too _____.
能給我換個房間嗎？這兒太吵了。

2. My wife was woken up several times by the noise the baggage _____ made.
我妻子被運送行李的電梯發出的嘈雜聲弄醒了幾次。

3. She said it was too _____ for her.
她說這使她難以忍受。

4. I'm awfully _____, sir.
非常對不起，先生。

5. I do _____.
我向您道歉。

6. No _____, sir.
沒問題，先生。

7. We'll manage it, but we don't have any _____ room today.
我們會盡力辦到，但是今天我們沒有空餘房間。

8. Could you wait till _____?
等到明天好嗎？

9. I hope we'll be able to enjoy our stay in a quiet suite tomorrow evening and have a sound _____.
我希望明天晚上我們能呆在一套安靜的房間裡睡個好覺。

10. And if there is anything more you need, please let us _____.
如果還需要別的什麼東西，請告訴我們。

11. The _____ in this room is too dim.

這房間裡的燈光太暗了。

12. Please get me a _____ one.
請給我換個更亮的。

13. Certainly, sir. I'll be _____ right away.
好的，先生，我馬上就回來。

14. The room is too cold for me. I feel rather _____ when I sleep.
這房間太冷了，我睡覺時感到很冷。

15. We might have overlooked some _____.
我們可能忽略了一些細小的地方。

16. I'll look _____ this matter at once.
我馬上去查清這件事情。

17. There could have been some _____. I do apologize.
可能是出了什麼差錯，實在是對不起。

18. Our manager is not in town. Shall I get our _____ manager for you?
我們的經理不在本地。我幫您叫經理助理來好嗎？

19. To express our regret for all the _____, we offer you complimentary flowers.
我們給您帶來了這麼多麻煩，為表達歉意，特為您提供免費花籃。

20. Please allow me to _____ a chambermaid to your room to help you look for it again thoroughly.
請允許我派一個服務員來幫您在房間裡再仔細找找。

21. Shall I call the _____ for you?
我幫您報警好嗎？

II. *Make a dialogue according to the following situation.*（創作情景對話）

酒店誤安排給了之前來的另一位同姓名的客人了，此時房間已經客滿，酒店安排其到另一家酒店，並付給客人打車費。客人讓不滿意，要求給說法。請根據以上情景，創作一篇不少於100個單詞的英文對話。

Unit 7　Check-out　結帳退房

Background（背景知識）①

A hotel cashier collects money from guests for their lodging accommodations and any other

---

① 背景知識部分摘自網路，有改動。原文網址：https://careertrend.com/about-7230050-hotel-cashier-job-description.html

fees they may incur during their stay, including parking, valet, room service and telephone or computer use fees. She is also commonly required to maintain related records and files regarding financial transactions that take place at the front desk. Her job normally entails answering guest inquiries regarding fees and services.

Good mathematical skills are required for this job. Although most modern cash registers or point-of-sale (POS) terminals automatically calculate fees and taxes based on the programming of their software, a hotel cashier is expected to be able to accurately calculate bulk room rates or corporate discounts and add up room and auxiliary charges utilizing a calculator or adding machine. Customer service skills are needed for this job, as well as the ability to work well with other hotel staff personnel.

Besides processing cash, debit card and credit card transactions for guests, a hotel cashier is often responsible for preparing and submitting daily bank deposits. He may also be required to accurately complete sales tax reporting forms. If customers have questions or concerns about charges on their bills, the hotel cashier should be competent in addressing them to their satisfaction. If a hotel has safes or safe-deposit boxes to protect valuable possessions of their guests, the hotel cashier is frequently in charge of guaranteeing the security of the contents.

Situational dialogues (情景對話)

Dialogue 1

C—Cashier   G—Guest

C: Good morning. Can I help you?

G: Yes, I'd like to check out.

C: May I have you name and your room number, please?

G: Mr. Mario in Room 714.

C: Hold on, please. Okay, Mr. Mario. It's 200 dollars. How would you like to pay?

G: By my Visa card. Do you need the card?

C: Yes, please. Let me print out the receipt for you. Here is your bill. A double room for two nights. If everything is okay, would you please sign here?

G: Uh…what is this charge for?

C: Let me see…I am sorry. That is my fault. This is the room service you asked for.

G: Oh, that's right. Here you go.

C: Thank you for staying at Beijing Hotel. I hope you will come to our hotel again. Would you like me to call a taxi for you?

G: Yes. I'd appreciate it.

C: Have a nice day!

G: Thanks. The same to you.

Translation（譯文）

C——收銀員　G——客人

C: 早上好。需要幫助嗎？

G: 是的，我想退房。

C: 請問一下您的姓名和房號？

G: 馬里奧先生，714 房間。

C: 請稍等。好，馬里奧先生，費用是 200 美元。您想如何付款呢？

G: 用我的維薩卡。你需要卡嗎？

C: 是的，麻煩您。我來為你打印收據。這是您的帳單。一個雙人間，兩個晚上。如果沒問題，您能在這裡簽名嗎？

G: 嗯……這是什麼費用？

C: 讓我看看……很抱歉，這是我的錯。這是您要的客房送餐服務。

G: 哦，沒錯。給你。

C: 謝謝您下塌北京飯店。希望您下次再來光臨我們酒店。您需要我叫一輛出租車嗎？

G: 是的。謝謝。

C: 祝您愉快！

G: 謝謝。你也一樣。

Words and expressions（單詞和短語）

check-out 結帳退房

Visa card 維薩卡

print 打印

charge 費用

fault 錯

appreciate 感謝

Dialogue 2

C—Cashier　G—Guest

C: Good morning, sir. What can I do for you?

G: I'm leaving at 11：00, so I'd like to settle my account now.

C: Yes, sir. May I have your room number?

G: Room 523, and the name is Samuel Edgar.

C: Right. Please just wait a moment. I'll get your bill ready for you right away.

G：Thanks.

C：Have you used your mini bar since breakfast?

G：No, I haven't.

C：Well, sir. Here's your bill. Please check and sign it.

G：I'd like to settle my account with my credit card. What credit cards do you accept?

C：We accept Master card and Visa.

G：Do you accept American Express?

C：I'm very sorry, we don't.

G：Ah, I only have American Express. I'll have to pay in cash. Here you are.

C：Thank you, Mr. Edgar. Here's your receipt. I hope you enjoyed your stay.

G：Yes, your service was wonderful. I did enjoy staying here.

C：I'm glad to hear that. I hope you'll come again.

Translation（譯文）

C——收銀員　G——客人

C：早上好，先生。我能為您做什麼嗎？

G：我要在11點離店，所以現在想結帳。

C：好的，先生。能告訴我您的房號嗎？

G：523房間，我叫塞繆爾·埃德加。

C：對的。請稍等。我馬上為您準備好帳單。

G：謝謝。

C：早餐之後您使用過小冰箱嗎？

G：沒有。

C：好的，先生。這是您的帳單。請檢查並簽字。

G：我想用信用卡結帳。你們接受什麼信用卡？

C：我們接受萬事達卡和維薩卡。

G：美國運通呢？

C：很抱歉，不接受。

G：哦，我只有美國運通，只能現金支付了。給你。

C：謝謝你，埃德加先生。這是您的收據。希望您在本店住得開心。

G：是，你的服務很棒。我確實喜歡住在這裡。

C：我很高興。希望您能再次下榻。

Words and expressions（單詞和短語）

cashier 出納員

settle account 結帳，買單

right away 馬上
mini bar 小冰箱
breakfast 早餐
Master card 萬事達卡
American Express 美國運通

Dialogue 3

C—Cashier　G—Guest

C：Good morning. Can I help you?

G：Yes. I want to check out and change some US dollars into Chinese RMB.

C：How much is that?

G：200 US dollars. Here you are.

C：We change foreign currencies according to today's exchange rate... 100 US dollars is an equivalent of RMB 700.

G：OK, I'll take it.

C：Please fill in the exchange memo, your passport number and the total sum, and sign your name.

G：Here you are. Is that all right?

C：Yes, thanks. What denomination do you need?

G：Give me 40 five-yuan notes, 10 ten-yuan notes, and all 100-yuan notes for the rest.

C：Certainly. Here is RMB1,400. Check it please and keep the memo.

G：All right. Thank you for your help.

C：Always at your service.

Translation（譯文）

C——收銀員　G——客人

C：早上好。您需要幫助嗎？

G：是的。我想退房，還要把一些美元兌換成人民幣。

C：有多少？

G：200 美元。給你。

C：我們按今天的匯率兌換外匯……100 美元相當於 700 元人民幣。

G：好，換吧。

C：請填寫外匯兌換水單，您的護照號碼和總金額。並簽您的名字。

G：給你。填對了嗎？

C：是的，謝謝。您需要什麼面額的紙幣？

G：請給我 5 元紙幣 40 張，10 元紙幣 10 張，其餘的都給 100 元面額的。

C：好的。這是 1,400 元人民幣。請點一下，並收好水單。

G：好的。謝謝你的幫助。

C：隨時為您服務。

Words and expressions（單詞和短語）

change 換

foreign 外國的

currency 貨幣

according to 根據

exchange rate 匯率

equivalent 等價物

memo 水單

passport 護照

total sum 總額

denomination 幣值的單位

note 紙幣

Exercises（練習題）

I. Complete the sentences.（補全句子）

1. I'd like to pay my _____ now.
我想現在結帳。

2. Your name and room _____, please?
請問您的姓名和房間號碼？

3. Have you _____ any hotel services this morning?
請問您今天早晨是否用過旅館內的服務設施？

4. Four nights at 90 US dollors each, and here are the meals that you had at the hotel. That makes a _____ of 665 US dollars.
4 個晚上，每晚 90 美元，加上膳食費，總共是 660 美元。

5. Can I pay by _____ card?
我可以用信用卡支付嗎？

6. Please _____ your name here.
請您在這裡簽名。

7. Excuse me. We're leaving _____. I'd like to pay our bills now.
勞駕。我們今天要離去了。我希望現在就把帳結清。

8. By the way, I'd like to tell you that the _____ time is 12：00, sir.
先生，順便告訴您，結帳後離開旅館時間是12點。

9. How about the _____ for the days you shared the room with your friend?
這幾天您的朋友與您同住產生的費用怎麼辦呢？

10. Please add to my _____.
請記在我的帳裡。

11. Have you used any hotel services this morning or had _____ at the hotel dining room, Mr. Green?
格林先生，今天早晨您是否用過旅館服務設施，或在旅館餐廳用過早餐？

12. The _____ for the eight days is five hundred sixty yuan and eighty fen.
8天費用總計是560元8角。

13. Here is your bill, two twin rooms for four nights at ＄400. The _____ that you had at the hotel are ＄120. That makes a total at ＄520.
這是您的帳單，兩個雙人房間，四個晚上，400美元，餐廳用餐的餐費是120美元，一共520美元。

14. You can use the room _____ four o'clock.
您可以使用這個房間到4點。

15. Just a moment, please. The _____ will have your bill ready in a moment.
請稍等，收銀員馬上會準備好您的帳單。

16. I'm afraid this _____ is not accepted in our hotel.
恐怕我們酒店不收這種貨幣。

17. If you think _____ is any error in your bill, we can check it again for you.
如果您認為帳目有錯，我們可以為您核對一下。

18. Would you like to settle the _____ in cash?
您願意用現金支付差額嗎？

19. Here is your _____. We look forward to serving you again.
這是您的收據，我們期待能再次為您服務。

20. I'm afraid we have no credit arrangements with your _____, sir. You may pay by any of these credit cards, instead.
先生，恐怕我們與貴公司沒有信用貸款的協定，您可以改用任何一種信用卡付款。

II. Make a dialogue according to the following situation. （創作情景對話）

客人B要辦理退房，服務員A收取客人的房卡和押金單，核對客人房號。通知客房服務員查房，辦理結帳手續，詢問客人結帳方式，系統結帳，打結帳單，請客人簽字等。請根據以上情景，創作一篇不少於100個單詞的英文對話。

Chapter Two　　Housekeeping 客房部

Unit 1　Showing Room　介紹客房

Background（背景知識）

Housekeeping Department is one of the main operational department of a hotel. Itprincipally pay more attention to the sanitation of chambers and public areas, and supply comfortable and satisfying housekeeping facilities for guests. When guests walk into bright, clean room, they are quite pleased and feel at home. Guests will get their first impression of the hotel's living circumstances when the room attendant shows the room. Consequently, housekeeping staff should work with enthusiasm, initiative patience and thoughtfulness.

Situational dialogues（情景對話）

Dialogue 1

B—Bellboy　G—Guest

(The bellboy shows the guest into his room.)

B: This way, please.

B: This is your room. Here are your keys.

G: It is a lovely room.

B: Where can I put your luggage?

G: Just here. Thank you.

B: (Pointing to the bedside control) And over here, sir, are the switches for the bedside lamps. This is the volume control for the radio, and this is the channel selector.

G: What about the TV?

B: Over here, sir. This is the remote control. There are eight channels, including two English programs. Here is a program guide.

G: I see.

B: And over there, sir, is the balcony.

G: Oh, It looks a good view.

B: And behind me is the bathroom.

G: Fine. By the way, is your water safe?

B: There is distilled water in the mini-bar over there. And here is our service guide.

G: Thank you very much.

Translation（譯文）

B—行李員　G—客人

（行李員引領客人進入房間。）

B：這邊請。

B：這是您的房間。這是您的鑰匙。

G：好可愛的房間。

B：您的行李我放在哪裡呢？

G：就放在這裡。謝謝！

B：（指著床頭控制面板）先生，這裡是床頭燈的開關。這是收音機的音量控制，這是頻道選擇器。

G：電視呢？

B：在這裡，先生。這是遙控器。有八個頻道，包括兩個英語節目。這是節目指南。

G：明白了。

B：先生，那邊是陽臺。

G：噢，看起來景色很美。

B：我身後是浴室。

G：好的。順便問一下，你們的水可以飲用嗎？

B：那邊的小冰箱有蒸餾水。這是我們的服務指南。

G：非常感謝。

Words and expressions（單詞和短語）

bellboy 行李員

lovely 可愛的

luggage 行李

bedside 床頭的

control 控制

switch 開關

lamp 燈

volume 音量

radio 廣播

channel 頻道

selector 選擇器

remote control 遙控器

program 節目

guide 向導

balcony 陽臺

view 風景

safe 安全的

distilled water 蒸餾水

service guide 服務指南

Dialogue 2

B—Bellboy　G—Guest

B：After you, sir. Shall I draw back the curtains for you?

G：Yes, please. Would you please show me how to operate these devices?

B：Certainly. This is the temperature control of the air-conditioner. You can adjust temperature with it.

G：And what is this remote for?

B：That's the remote control for the television. Just press the button on the lower right corner if you want to turn it on.

G：I see.

Translation（譯文）

B——行李員　G——客人

B：您先請，先生。您需要拉開窗簾嗎？

G：是的，麻煩你了。請告訴我如何操作這些設備好嗎？

B：當然可以。這是空調的溫度控制。您可以用它調整溫度。

G：這個遙控器是幹什麼用的呢？

B：這是電視的遙控器。如果您想打開電視，只需按下右下角的按鈕就行。

G：我明白了。

Words and expressions（單詞和短語）

curtain 窗簾

operate 操作

device 裝置

temperature 溫度

air-conditioner 空調器

adjust 調整

television 電視

press 壓；按

button 按鈕

corner 角落

Dialogue 3

B—Bellboy　G—Guest

B：Here's your room, sir. After you, please.

G：Thank you. The room is beautiful.

B：I'm glad you like it

G：How can I make coffee?

B：You can make your coffee by using electric kettle here. The coffee and tea bag in the refrigerator are free of charge.

G：Really? What about these yogurts and fruits? Are they free too?

B：No, sir. They will be charged when you check out.

G：I see. What's that on the ceiling?

B：It's a smoke detector. Please don't smoke in the room, sir. Or the smoke will trigger alarms.

G：What if I want to smoke?

B：There is a smoking section at the corner of the corridor.

G：Thank you.

Translation（譯文）

B——行李員　G——客人

B：這是您的房間，先生。您先請。

G：謝謝你！房間很漂亮。

B：很高興您喜歡它。

G：我怎麼煮咖啡呢?

B：您可以用這裡的電熱水壺製作咖啡。冰箱裡的咖啡和茶袋都是免費的。

G：真的嗎? 這些酸奶和水果呢? 也是免費的嗎?

B：不是的，先生。您結帳時需要支付它們的費用。

G：明白了。天花板上那是什麼?

B：這是菸霧探測器。請不要在房間裡抽菸，先生。否則菸霧會觸發警報。

G：如果我想要抽菸怎麼辦？

B：在走廊的拐角處有一個吸菸區。

G：謝謝你！

Words and expressions（單詞和短語）

electric kettle 電水壺

refrigerator 冰箱

yogurt 酸奶

fruit 水果

check out 退房

ceiling 天花板

smoke 菸霧

detector 探測器

trigger 引發

alarm 警報

section 部分

corridor 走廊

Dialogue 4

C—Clerk　G—Guest

C：（Knocking at the door and waiting for a reply）Room attendant, may I come in?

G：Yes. Come in, please.

C：Good afternoon, Mr. Black. Here is the transformer you need.

G：Thank you. By the way, we'd like to have breakfast in our room. When should we order that?

C：This is your doorknob menu. Just check the items you would like for breakfast, mark down the time and hang it outside your door before you go to bed tonight. Our hotel has very considerate room service.

G：I hope I'll get up on time.

C：You can place a wake-up call with the operator.

G：Thank you for the information.

C：If you don't want to be disturbed, just hang the「DND」sign on the doorknob or push the red button. If it is turned the other way, I'll know you want me to make up your room.

G：That's very kind of you.

C: I'm always at your service.

Translation（譯文）

C——職員　G——客人

C：（敲門，等待回復）客房服務員，我可以進來嗎？

G：請進。

C：下午好，布萊克先生。這是您要的變壓器。

G：謝謝你。順便問一下，我們想在房間裡用早餐。應該怎樣訂餐呢？

C：這是您的門把手菜單。只需要把要點的項目打勾，記下時間，然後今晚睡覺前把菜單掛在您的門外。我們的酒店提供非常周到的客房送餐服務。

G：我希望能準時起床。

C：您可以與接線員登記叫醒服務。

G：謝謝你的回答。

C：如果您不想被打擾，就把「DND」的牌子掛在門把手上，或者按下紅色按鈕。如果牌子掛反面，我就知道您需要整理房間。

G：你太好了。

C：隨時為您效勞。

Words and expressions（單詞和短語）

room attendant 服務員

transformer 變壓器

order 訂

doorknob 門把

menu 菜單

item 項目

mark 作記號於

considerate 考慮周到的

room service 客房送餐服務

get up 起床

on time 按時

wake-up call 叫醒電話

operator 接線員

disturb 打擾

push 壓

button 按鍵

make up 整理

at your service 為您服務

Notes：

room attendant：客房服務員

doorknob menu：門把菜單，掛門餐牌

wake-up call：喚醒電話，叫早

DND：請勿打擾＝do not disturb

I'm always at your service. 我們隨時為您服務。

Exercises（練習題）

I. Complete the sentences.（補全句子）

1. Your room is _____ the sea. It's very beautiful. I hope you will like it.
您的房間正好面對大海，非常美麗。我希望您會喜歡。

2. Mr. White, here is the light switch, the wardrobe, and the _____.
懷特先生，這是燈具開關、衣櫃和小冰櫃。

3. Here is the master switch. This is the temperature _____.
這是總開關。這是溫度控制器。

4. I feel like taking a bath to fresh up after the international _____.
經過跨洋飛行以後，我很想洗個澡來恢復一下精神。

5. This is the _____ control.
這是遙控器。

6. By the way, is the tap water _____?
順便問一句，這兒的自來水能喝嗎？

7. There are two bottles of drinking water in the bathroom, _____ of charge.
浴室有兩瓶飲用水，都是免費的。

8. If you need anything else, please dial 8. We're always _____ your service.
如果您有什麼事，請撥「8」號鍵。我們隨時會為您服務。

9. I hope you will enjoy your _____ with us.
有事情隨時叫我。預祝您在我們這裡度過愉快的時光。

10. Here is our hotel's Service Information Booklet. It gives you an idea about our services and _____.
這是我們飯店的服務指南，內有飯店服務及設施介紹。

11. Welcome to the eleventh floor. I'm the floor _____.
歡迎入住十一樓，我是樓層服務員。

12. This way, please. I'll _____ you to your room.

這邊請。我帶您到客房。

13. How do you _____ this room?
您認為這個房間怎樣？

14. The room is _____ south and commands a good view of the beautiful garden.
這個房間朝南，能看到花園裡的美景。

15. If you want to make an _____ call, please dial「0」first.
如果您想撥打外線，請先撥零。

16. If you need help, please _____「9」.
如果您需要我們服務，請撥打電話「9」。

17. There is a telephone _____ on the writing desk.
寫字臺上有一本電話簿。

18. There are twenty _____ including three English programs.
一共有二十個頻道，其中包括三個英語頻道。

19. I'll get the _____ for you. They are in the bedside table.
我給您拿拖鞋，在床頭櫃裡。

20. Here is the light _____.
這是電燈開關。

21. I'll bring you one _____.
我馬上給您拿來。

22. Be sure not to forget the _____ you set.
千萬別忘了您設置的密碼。

23. The _____ code is your room number.
原始密碼是您的房間號碼。

24. The _____ will not unlock if you put in the wrong password.
如果輸入錯誤的密碼，保險箱不會打開。

25. _____ it will cause much trouble.
否則就麻煩了。

II. Make a dialogue according to the following situation. (創作情景對話)

服務員詢問客人的房間號，確認客房的房間後，並說「您這邊請」，引領賓客進入房間內，為客人介紹：空調開關、熱水壺、服務指南、酒店特色服務及服務電話號碼等。請根據以上情景，創作一篇不少於100個單詞的英文對話。

Unit 2　Cleaning Room　客房清理

Background（背景知識）

The room attendant performs routine duties in cleaning and servicing of guest rooms and baths under supervision of housekeeping supervisor. Room attendant promotes a positive image of the property to guests and must be pleasant, honest, friendly and should also able to address guest requests and problems.

He/She should maintain complete knowledge of and comply with all housekeeping departmental policies/service and also the hotel's procedures/standards. Additionally, maintain complete knowledge of correct maintenance and use of equipment.

Situational dialogues（情景對話）

Dialogue 1

R—Room Attendant　　G—Guest

R: Housekeeping. May I come in?

G: Yes, please.

R: Good morning, sir. Sorry to disturb you. May I clean the room now?

G: Ok.

R: Do you mind my opening the window?

G: No, of course not.

R: Oh, sir. I'm afraid you have not marked the minibar list. You had a Brandy at costs RMB 100. Am I correct?

G: Yes, exactly.

R: Would you please sign your name on the minibar list?

G: Sure. ... Here you are. By the way, the minibar doesn't keep cool.

R: Oh, sorry. Let me have a check…Ah, the plug is not tightly inserted into the socket. Would you like me to tidy up a bit in the bathroom?

G: Ok. But please don't use the vacuum cleaner anywhere in the room.

R: I see.

(After the cleaning)

R: Is there anything else I can do for you, sir?

G: No, thank you. I really appreciate your efficient work.

R: My pleasure. Goodbye.

Translation（譯文）

R——客房服務員　G——客人

R：客房服務員。我可以進來嗎？

G：可以，請進。

R：早上好，先生。對不起，打擾您了。我現在可以打掃房間嗎？

G：好的。

R：您介意我打開窗戶嗎？

G：當然不會。

R：哦，先生，您好象沒有標記小冰箱清單。您喝過一瓶售價100元的白蘭地，對嗎？

G：是的，沒錯。

R：請在小冰箱清單簽上您的名字好嗎？

G：當然……給你。順便說一下，小冰箱不制冷。

R：哦，抱歉。讓我看一下……哦，插頭沒有插緊。您需要我收拾一下浴室嗎？

G：好的。但請不要在房間的任何地方使用吸塵器。

R：明白了。

（清潔過後）

R：先生，還有什麼需要嗎？

G：不用了，謝謝。非常感謝你高效的工作。

R：不客氣。再見。

Words and expressions（單詞和短語）

disturb 打擾

mind 介意

brandy 白蘭地

correct 正確的

exactly 確切地

sign 簽字

by the way 順便問一下

here you are 給您

plug 插頭

tightly 插緊地

insert 插入

socket 插座

tidy up 整理，打掃

vacuum cleaner 吸塵器

appreciate 感謝

efficient 高效的

Dialogue 2

R—Room Attendant　G—Guest

R：Good evening, housekeeping. May I come in?

G：Yes, please.

R：May I do the turn-down service now, sir?

G：What is that?

R：I will take away the bed cover, fold back the duvet and leave some chocolate on the pillows. Finally I will tidy up the bathroom and refresh the supplies.

G：Oh, I see. Could you come at 10? My friends are coming for a visit.

R：Very well.

G：But can you clean the bathroom now? I've just had a shower. It's in a mess.

R：Certainly, sir. I will finish cleaning it in 10 minutes.

G：Thank you.

Translation（譯文）

R——客房服務員　G——客人

R：晚上好，客房服務員。我可以進來嗎？

G：可以的，請進。

R：先生，現在可以為您開夜床了嗎？

G：那是什麼？

R：我會帶走床罩，反折羽絨被，並在枕頭上放一些巧克力。最後我會整理浴室，並更新用品。

G：好，我明白了。你能10點過來嗎？我的朋友們準備來拜訪。

R：好的。

G：但是你現在可以打掃衛生間嗎？我剛洗了個澡。裡面很亂。

R：當然可以，先生。我會在10分鐘後完成清洗。

G：謝謝你！

Words and expressions（單詞和短語）

turn-down service 開夜床服務

bed cover 床罩

fold 折

duvet 羽絨被

chocolate 巧克力

pillow 枕頭

finally 最後

refresh 更新

shower 淋浴

mess 混亂

Dialogue 3

H—Housekeeper　G—Guest

H: Good morning, Mr. and Mrs. Ogden. May I come through, please?

G: Good morning? It's almost noon, and our room hasn't been made up yet.

H: I'm so sorry, madam and sir. I was just coming along to your room as soon as I have finished this one.

G: Really? I do think you could do our room first for a change. Why are we always the last?

H: Well, I have a section of 15 rooms, and I always do the check-out rooms first, unless there is a request.

G: Check-out rooms? What are they? Do you mean that the people who go out early get their rooms done first? If so, we were out at 7: 00 a.m. this morning.

H: A check-out room means the guests are leaving the hotel at the end of their stay. We have to get the rooms ready for sale by the Front Office.

G: But we'd like to take a nap after lunch.

H: Well, I see. Your room will be ready in half an hour, Mr. and Mrs. Bellow, after your lunch.

G: Can you do this for us every day?

H: Certainly, madam. We always try to have rooms made up early on request. Just let us know what you need, and if we can, we'll oblige.

G: Thank you. I suppose there is a lot of work for you. Is the hotel full?

H: Yes, sir. The occupancy is very high. This is the peak season for tourism in this area.

G: Thank you for your cooperation.

H: My pleasure. I do hope you are enjoying your stay with us.

G: Oh, we are. Good bye.

Translation（譯文）

H——客房服務員　G——客人

H：早上好，奧格登先生和太太。請讓我過去一下好嗎？

G：早上好？都快中午了，我們的房間還沒有收拾好。

H：對不起，夫人，先生。我完成這間房後，就馬上到你們的房間。

G：真的嗎？我認為你可以先收拾我們的房間。為什麼我們總是最後一間呢？

H：哦，我負責一段15個房間的區域，我總是先做走客房，除非另有要求。

G：走客房？是什麼意思？你是說出去早的人，你們會優先收拾他們的房間嗎？如果是這樣的話，我們今天早上7：00就出門了。

H：走客房是指著客人住店末期要離店了。我們必須把房間準備好，給前廳出租。

G：但是我們想在午飯後打個盹。

H：好的，我明白了。你們的房間會在半小時後收拾好，就在你們午餐後，奧格登先生和夫人。

G：你能每天這樣幫我們收拾嗎？

H：當然可以，夫人。我們總是盡量按照要求早點收拾房間。只要你們提出需求，如果可以，我們會滿足。

G：謝謝你。我估計你有大量的工作要做。酒店滿客了嗎？

H：是的，先生。入住率很高。這是本地區的旅遊旺季。

G：謝謝你的合作。

H：不客氣。希望您住店愉快。

G：嗯，我們住得很開心。再見。

Words and expressions（單詞和短語）

for a change 改變一下

check out room 走客房

request 請求

Front Office 前廳部

nap 小睡

lunch 午餐

oblige 服從，幫忙

suppose 猜想

occupancy 入住率

peak season 旺季

tourism 旅遊

cooperation 配合

Dialogue 4

C—Clerk   G—Guest

C: Good morning. Room Center. How may I help you?

G: Good morning. Could you send someone to clean my room?

C: May I have your name and room number, please?

G: Malachi Angus. Room 2608.

C: Yes, Mr. Angus. The「DND」sign was hanged on your room doorknob most of the day. So we didn't clean the room so as not to disturb you.

G: Well, it is my fault. I forgot to take down the sign when I went out.

C: Do you wish the room to be cleaned now?

G: Yes, if there is not much bother.

C: No trouble at all, sir. The room attendant will be in your room soon.

(A few minutes later)

C: Housekeeping. May I come in?

G: Yes, please.

C: Good morning, Mr. Angus. I'm here to clean the room. Do you mind my opening the window?

G: No, of course not.

Translation (譯文)

C——職員　G——客人

C：早上好。房務中心。我能為您服務嗎？

G：早上好。你能派人來打掃我的房間嗎？

C：麻煩說下你的名字和房號。

G：馬拉基·安格斯。2608 房間。

C：好的，安格斯先生。今天的大部分時間你的房間門把手都掛著「DND」標牌。所以我們沒有打掃房間，以免打擾你。

G：是我的錯。我走時忘了把標牌拿下。

C：您希望現在打掃房間嗎？

G：是的，如果方便的話。

C：沒事的，先生。客房服務員很快就會到您的房間。

（幾分鐘後）

C：客房服務員。我可以進來嗎？

G：請進。

C：早上好，安格斯先生。我來打掃房間。您介意我開窗嗎？
G：當然不介意。

Words and expressions（單詞和短語）

DND 請勿打擾（do not disturb）

doorknob 門把手

so as to 以便，以致

disturb 打擾

fault 錯

bother 麻煩

Exercises（練習題）

I. Complete the sentences.（補全句子）

1. What _____ would you like us to come back?
您希望我什麼時候再來？

2. Shall I come back _____, sir?
先生，我過會再來好嗎？

3. We will come and _____ your room immediately.
我們馬上就來打掃您的房間。

4. Your room will be _____ in half an hour.
您的房間過半小時就會打掃乾淨。

5. I'm afraid no cleaning can be done _____ 12：00 noon and 2：00 p. m. May we come between 2：00 p. m. and 3：00 p. m.？
恐怕，中午 12 點到下午 2 點期間我們不能打掃房間，我們在下午 2 點至 3 點之間打掃您的房間行嗎？

6. Just let us know what you need, and if we can, we will _____.
如果您需要什麼，就告訴我們，只要是做得到的，我們都會盡力為您效勞。

7. _____ service, may I come in? Good evening, sir.
開夜床服務，我可以進來嗎？晚上好，先生。

8. Please put out a「_____」sign on the door if you need to rest in the room, and the roommaids won't knock on the door again.
如果您需要在房間內休息，請在門上掛上「請勿打擾」牌，服務員就不會再敲門了。

9. Excuse me, sir, but I haven't finished cleaning your room. Shall I _____?
對不起，先生，我可以繼續清掃您的房間嗎？

10. I'm very _____, how long will it take you to finish your room?

我很累了，還需要多長時間你才能結束？

11. Certainly, would it be _____ if I return in half an hour?
當然可以，如您認為方便，我半小時後再來，可以嗎？

12. I'm sorry. I'm going to your room as _____ as I have finished this one.
對不起，我結束這間房後立即為您打掃。

13. Certainly, sir. I will clean up your room _____ tomorrow.
當然可以，先生，明天我將早點為您打掃房間。

14. _____. May I come in?
清掃客房，我可以進來嗎？

15. When would you like me to _____ your room, sir?
您要我什麼時間來給您打掃房間呢，先生？

16. Will it be _____ for you if I come to do your room in an hour?
一小時之後我再來清掃房間，方便嗎？

17. Your room will be ready before you come back from the restaurant, I _____.
我保證您就餐之後，房間一定清掃完畢。

18. I'm here to get your _____ cleaned.
我來打掃浴室。

19. I'll clean the bathroom and replace some fresh _____.
我會清掃浴室並換上新毛巾的。

20. The hotel provides free shoe _____ service for its guests.
飯店為住店客人提供免費擦鞋服務。

II. Make a dialogue according to the following situation. （創作情景對話）

客人 B 打電話到房務中心，要求服務員到客房打掃房間，說 10 點離開，下午 3 點回來。請服務員把房間內的書桌整理一下，衛生間打掃一下，垃圾清理一下等。請根據以上情景，創作一篇不少於 100 個單詞的英文對話。

Unit 3　Room Service　送餐服務

Background（背景知識）

In many hotels guests have a choice of having a breakfast and also often require their meals and drinks served in their room, perhaps by the same staff who serve in the restaurants and bars, or by the housekeeping staff, or by room (floor) service staff in a large hotel.

In some luxury hotels, room service is served almost around the clock, offering standard meals, between meal snacks, beverages and d'oeuvre for in-room entertainment and box lunches. Guests can place orders either through a telephone order-taker or through doorknob menus. Today room service in many hotels is only available for breakfast, and facilities for tea and coffee making within the room are more usually provided as an alternative.

For the hotel, room service is an additional product, which may relieve pressures in the restaurant and bars, and particularly through pre-ordered breakfasts and through room bar units, it may contribute to a more efficient food and beverage service.

Situational dialogues（情景對話）

Dialogue 1

A—Clerk　B—Guest

A: Good morning, room service. May I help you?

B: I'd like to have a meal in my room.

A: Certainly, sir. We offer two types of breakfast: American and continental. Which one would you prefer?

B: What does a continental breakfast have?

A: Chilled orange juice, toast with butter, coffee or tea.

B: That will be fine. I will take it. I'd like a white coffee with two sugars, please.

A: I see. May I have your name and room number, please?

B: Sure, it's Stephen Lee in room 1506.

A: Let me confirm your order: Mr. Stephen Lee in room 1506, Continental breakfast, white coffee with two sugars. Is that right?

B: Exactly.

A: Your order will be ready soon. Thank you for calling.

B: You can forget the sugar and the cream. Just plain coffee will do. And please make it very strong.

Translation（譯文）

A——職員　B——客人

A：早上好，客房送餐服務。需要幫忙嗎？

B：我想在房間裡用餐。

A：好的，先生。我們提供兩種類型的早餐：美式和歐陸式。您喜歡哪一種？

B：歐陸式早餐有什麼？

A：冷凍橙汁，吐司麵包配黃油，咖啡或茶。

B：很好。我就點這個吧。我想要一份加牛奶的咖啡和兩塊糖，謝謝。

A：我明白了。請說下您的名字和房號，好嗎？

B：斯蒂芬・李，1506 房間。

A：我來確認您的訂單：斯蒂芬・李，1506 房間，歐陸式早餐，一份加牛奶的咖啡和兩塊糖。是這樣嗎？

B：完全正確。

A：您的早餐很快就好。謝謝您的來電。

B：請不要放糖和奶油。純咖啡就可以了。而且要很濃。

Words and expressions（單詞和短語）

room service 客房送餐服務

meal 一餐飯

offer 供應

continental 大陸的

prefer 更喜歡

orange juice 橙汁

toast 吐司麵包

butter 黃油

white coffee 加牛奶的咖啡

confirm 確認

cream 奶油

strong 濃

Dialogue 2

R—Room Attendant　G—Guest

R：Good morning. Room service. May I help you?

G：Good morning. It's Mr. Wilmer in Room 1325. Can I have breakfast in my room tomorrow morning?

R：Certainly, Mr. Wilmer. Breakfast can be served in your room from seven o'clock until ten. Our hotel has very good room service.

G：When shall I order that?

R：You can use our doorknob menu if you like. Please check the items you would like to have for breakfast, mark down the time, and hang it outside your door before you go to bed.

G：Is there any other way to ask for room service?

R：Yes, Mr. Wilmer. You may have breakfast arranged by phone. Just dial「7」to call the

Room Service to order your breakfast, lunch and dinner.

G: Thank you for your information. By the way, what shall I do with the plates when I finish eating?

R: You may just leave them in the room or put them outside your door. We'll take care of it.

G: Oh, I see. Thank you very much.

R: You're welcome. Have a pleasant stay with us.

Translation（譯文）

R——客房服務員　G——客人

R：早上好。客房送餐服務。您需要幫忙嗎？

G：早上好。我是1325房間的威爾默先生。明天早上我可以在房間用早餐嗎？

R：當然可以，威爾默先生。早餐可以在7點到10點之間送到您的房間。我們酒店有很好的送餐服務。

G：什麼時候下單呢？

R：如果你願意，可以使用我們的門把手菜單。請勾選您想要的早餐項目，寫下時間，睡覺之前把它掛在您的房門外。

G：還有其他的客房送餐服務途徑嗎？

R：有的，威爾默先生。你可以在電話裡安排訂早餐。只要撥打「7」到客房送餐服務部來預訂你的早餐、午餐和晚餐。

G：謝謝你的回答。順便問一下，用餐過後，我該怎麼處理餐盤？

R：就放在房間裡就行，或者放在你的房門外。我們會收回的。

G：哦，我明白了。非常感謝。

R：不客氣。祝您住店愉快。

Words and expressions（單詞和短語）

certainly 當然

serve 端上，招待

arrange 安排

dial 撥打

plate 盤子

take care of 保管

pleasant 愉快

Dialogue 3

C—Clerk　G—Guest

C: Good afternoon, Room Service. What can I do for you?

R: Good afternoon. This is Mr. Fidel from Room 921. I am having a party in my room this evening. Can I arrange it through you?

C: Certainly. How many people are there in your party?

R: I am not sure. Perhaps 10.

C: May I suggest sirloin steak and pork chop?

R: Sounds great. I will have five sirloins and five porks.

C: Very well. Would you like something to drink?

R: I've got some whiskey, but I need some beer.

C: Certainly. Any dessert or salad?

R: Salad, please.

C: When will the party begin?

R: At seven.

C: I see.

Translation（譯文）

C——職員　G——客人

C：下午好，客房送餐服務。我能為您做什麼嗎？

G：下午好。我是921房間的菲德爾先生。我今天晚上在房間裡辦一個聚會。我可以麻煩你安排嗎？

C：當然可以。你們一共有幾位？

G：我不確定。也許10位。

C：我建議沙朗牛排和豬排，行嗎？

G：聽起來不錯。我要五個沙朗牛排和五個豬排。

C：好的。你們要來點酒水嗎？

G：我有一些威士忌，但我需要一些啤酒。

C：沒問題。需要甜點或沙拉嗎？

G：沙拉吧。

C：聚會什麼時候開始？

G：7點。

C：我明白了。

Words and expressions（單詞和短語）

sirloin steak 沙朗牛排

pork chop 豬排

dessert 甜點

salad 沙拉

Exercises（練習題）

I. Complete the sentences.（補全句子）

1. Would you _____ bring me some breakfast?
請為我送來一份早餐，好嗎？

2. At what _____ would you like your breakfast?
您希望什麼時候把您的早餐送來？

3. A _____ breakfast or American breakfast?
是要歐式早餐還是美式早餐？

4. With coffee or _____?
需要咖啡還是茶？

5. For how _____ people, please?
請問要幾個人的送餐？

6. I will bring it up right _____.
我馬上把它送上來。

7. Good morning, here is the Continental breakfast you _____.
早上好，這是您點的歐式早餐。

8. Would you like to have something else _____ the Continental breakfast?
除了歐式早餐，您還想要點別的嗎？

9. Would you please sign the _____?
請您在帳單上簽名好嗎？

10. Thank you, _____ your breakfast please, good-bye.
謝謝，請慢用，再見。

11. It won't take long to _____ for your breakfast.
您的早餐不會用太長時間準備。

12. Please _____ your name and room number here on the bill.
請在帳單上簽上您的名字和房間號。

13. I would like some _____ now.
我想現在進午餐。

14. It is _____ Service here.
這是送餐服務。

15. Shall I _____ you some coffee now?
我可以為您倒一杯咖啡嗎？

16. Your food and _____ will be sent up in a few minutes.

您要的食品和飲料過幾分鐘就會送上去。
17. It will _____ only five minutes to send to your room.
只需五分鐘就可以送至您的房間。
18. I will send someone up _____ your breakfast immediately.
我馬上叫人把您的早餐送上來。
19. Our room service starts serving _____ 7 o'clock.
送餐服務從 7 點開始。
20. I am sorry, we don't start serving lunch _____ 11 a.m.
對不起，我們要上午 11 點菜開始提供午餐服務。
21. Is _____ anything else that you want?
您是不是還要點別的什麼？
22. The room service _____ is on the back of the door.
送餐服務菜單掛在門後。
23. It's my wife's _____ today. I'd like to order a cake.
今天是我太太的生日，我想訂一個蛋糕。
24. We have different sizes, 7inches, 9 inches and 11 inches, which do you _____?
我們有不同尺寸的蛋糕，有 7 英吋的、9 英吋的和 11 英吋的，你想要那一種？
25. Your breakfast will be sent to your room at exactly half _____ seven.
我們會在 7 點半將早餐送到您房間。
26. Can I have my breakfast _____ to the room?
我可以在房間用早餐嗎？
27. Some porridge, some fried eggs and some toast with jam and _____.
一些麥片粥，一份煎雞蛋，一份烤麵包和一些果醬、黃油。
28. How many eggs and how would you like them _____?
您要幾個雞蛋？幾成熟？
29. Could you bring me a _____ of milk and a boiled egg?
你能給我拿一杯牛奶和一個煮雞蛋嗎？
30. When couldI take away the _____ and glasses?
我何時來撤走餐盤和玻璃杯？
31. If you need, please dial「7」to the room service and we will _____ you anytime.
如果您需要什麼，請撥打電話「7」客房送餐服務，我們隨時為您服務。

II. Make a dialogue according to the following situation.（創作情景對話）
客人 B 打電話到餐飲部想讓送餐服務，服務員 C 禮貌回答有什麼食物提供，然後付費方式，價格是餐飲價格加 15%的服務費。然後客人 B 要一份拉面，一份叉燒，一杯橙汁。

送餐到客人房間門口時，敲門，然後告訴客人1.5個小時後回來去餐盤，放在門外就好。請根據以上情景，創作一篇不少於100個單詞的英文對話。

Unit 4　Laundry Service　洗衣服務

Background（背景知識）

Almost every star hotel provides laundry service, which provides quick and efficient service for the guests who need their clothes washed or pressed. Generally, there are laundry bags in the wardrobe. The clothes to be washed should be put in the bags and they are picked by room attendants. Room attendants should count the pieces of articles and ask guests to sign their names for confirmation. Meanwhile, guests can indicate some special instructions, such as stain removing, starching, sewing and mending, etc. Laundry service can be divided into regular service and express service according to the duration. There is a surcharge for express service.

Situational dialogues（情景對話）

Dialogue 1

C—Clerk　G—Guest

C: Excuse me. Have you any laundry? The laundry man is here to collect it.

G: No, not now, thank you.

C: If you have any, please just leave it in the laundry bag behind the bathroom door. The laundry man comes over to collect it every morning.

G: Thank you.

C: Please tell us or notify in the list whether you need your clothes ironed, washed, dry-cleaned or mended and also what time you want to get them back.

G: I see. What if there is any laundry damage? I wonder if your hotel has a policy on dealing with it.

C: In such a case, the hotel should certainly pay for it. The indemnity shall not exceed ten times of the laundry fee.

G: That sounds quite reasonable. I hope there's no damage at all.

C: Don't worry, sir. The Laundry Department has wide experience in their work.

G: All right. Thank you for your information.

C: You are welcome.

Translation（譯文）

C——職員　G——客人

C：打擾一下，您有要洗的衣物嗎？洗衣工過來收取。

G：現在沒有，謝謝。

C：如果有，請把它們放在浴室門後面的洗衣袋裡。洗衣工每天早上會過來收取。

G：謝謝。

C：請告訴我們或在洗衣單上寫明您的衣物是否需要熨燙，水洗，干洗或縫補，還要寫明何時需要取回衣物。

G：我明白了。如果你們洗壞了衣物怎麼辦？請問你們酒店是否有應對方案。

C：那樣的話，酒店當然應該賠償。賠償金不超過洗滌費的十倍。

G：聽起來很合理。我希望不會有損壞。

C：別擔心，先生。洗衣部有豐富的業務經驗。

G：好的。謝謝你的介紹。

C：不客氣。

Words and expressions（單詞和短語）

laundry 待洗衣物

collect 收集

laundry bag 洗衣袋

laundry man 洗衣工

notify 通知

iron 熨

dry-clean 干洗

mend 修補

damage 損壞

wonder 想知道

policy 政策

deal with 處理

in such a case 在這種情況下

indemnity 賠償

exceed 超過

laundry fee 洗滌費

reasonable 合理的

experience 經驗

Dialogue 2

S—Staff member   G—Guest

S：Laundry Service. May I help you?

G：Yes. I'm Miss Juliet in room 3004. I have a few laundries.

S：The room attendant will come to your room in five minutes to pick up your laundry.

G：Thank you. The thing is, I need my formal dress to be ready before 7：00 p.m. tonight.

S：I'm afraid you have to choose express service.

G：What's the difference?

S：We charge 50% extra for the express service, but your laundry will be ready within four hours.

G：Alright then.

Translation（譯文）

S——員工   G——客人

S：洗衣房。有什麼需要幫助嗎？

G：是的。我是3004房間的朱麗葉小姐。我有一些衣物要送洗。

S：客房服務員五分鐘後會來您的房間取走衣物。

G：謝謝你！問題是，我需要在今晚7點之前把禮服洗好。

S：恐怕你只能選擇快洗服務了。

G：有什麼區別呢？

S：快洗服務我們多收50%的費用，但是你的衣物將在四小時內洗好。

G：那好吧。

Words and expressions（單詞和短語）

room attendant 客房服務員

pick up 收取

formal dress 禮服

express service 快洗服務

charge 收費

Dialogue 3

S—Staff member   G—Guest

S：Good evening, this is Laundry Center. May I help you?

G：Yes, I'm Mrs. Aldo in Room 1516. I just received my laundry and I had a lot of complaints.

S：What is the problem, madam?

G: First, I sent a sweater to the laundry, but it came back badly shrunk. You must have washed it in very hot water. And I also sent a silk dress which was a little bit burnt.

S: I'm sorry you didn't enjoy our usual good service. In such a case, the hotel should certainly pay for the damage.

G: How can I get the compensation?

S: According to the hotel policies, we pay an indemnity no more than 10 times the laundry charge. I hope you can understand us.

G: What's the laundry charge, then?

S: A total of RMB 60.

G: RMB 60? It means I can only get RMB 600 for compensation. That's unfair.

S: We do apologize for all the inconvenience, madam. But it is the regulation.

G: Can it be RMB 1,000?

S: If you insist on that amount, I'll get the manager to talk to you.

G: I hope so.

S: I'll do my best to help you, madam. Please wait a moment. See you later.

Translation（譯文）

S——員工　G——客人

S：晚上好，這是洗衣中心。請問需要幫助嗎？

G：是的，我是1516房間的奧爾多太太。我剛收到我的衣服，要投訴你們。

S：發生什麼事了，夫人？

G：首先，我有一件毛衣拿去洗，但送回來時嚴重縮水。你們一定是用很熱的水來洗的。我還送洗了一件絲綢禮服，但是有點燒焦了。

S：很抱歉您沒能享受我們一貫的良好服務。這樣的話，酒店當然應該賠償您的損失。

G：我怎樣得到賠款？

S：根據酒店規定，我們支付的賠款不超過洗衣費的十倍。希望您能理解。

G：那麼，洗衣費是多少呢？

S：一共是60元。

G：60元？意思是我只能獲賠600元。這不公平。

S：我們為給您帶來的不便表示真誠道歉，夫人。但這是規定。

G：應該賠1000元吧？

S：如果您堅持這個數額，我找經理來和您談談。

G：我也這麼想。

S：我會盡力幫助你，夫人。請稍等一會兒。再見。

Chapter Two　Housekeeping 客房部

Words and expressions（單詞和短語）

receive 接收

complaint 投訴，抱怨

silk 絲綢

burn 燒焦

understand 理解

laundry charge 洗滌費用

compensation 賠償

unfair 不公平的

inconvenience 不便

regulation 規定

insist 堅持

Exercises（練習題）

I. Complete the sentences.（補全句子）

1. If your _____ is received before 10:00 a.m., we will deliver it to your room by 4:00 p.m. the same day.

如果您的衣服是在早上10點前送洗的，我們將在當天下午4點把衣服洗好送到您的房間。

2. If we receive your laundry before 3:00 p.m., we will get it back to you by _____ the next day.

如果您的衣服是下午3點送洗的，我們將在第二天中午前把您的衣服送回給您。

3. The laundry rate chart is contained in the stationery _____ in your dresser's drawer, sir.

洗衣價目表放在您梳妝臺抽屜的文具夾裡，先生。

4. Would you please send someone to room 502 to _____ up some laundry for me?

您可以派人到502房間來取一下我的送洗衣服嗎？

5. The roommaid will be there in a few _____.

服務員過幾分鐘就到您的房間來。

6. I have some _____ to be washed.

我有一些襯衣要洗。

7. Will tomorrow morning be all _____?

明天早上送給您行嗎？

8. I have a suit that I would like _____ before 7 o'clock this evening.

我有一套衣服想在今晚 7 點前燙好。

9. Could you fill out the laundry _____, please?
請您填一下這張洗衣單，好嗎？

10. The laundry form is in the _____ of the writing desk.
洗衣單放在寫字臺的抽屜裡。

11. Do you want these shirts _____, sir?
您想要這些襯衣上漿嗎，先生？

12. I'd like this sweater to be washed by hand in cold water; it might _____ otherwise.
我想這件毛衣要放在冷水中用手洗，否則它會縮水的。

13. By hand in cold water, I _____.
用冷水手洗，我明白了。

14. Could you send someone to _____ up my laundry, please?
您能派人來取一下我的送洗衣服嗎？

15. Certainly, madam. But I'm afraid it's too late for today's laundry. We can _____ it tomorrow around 4：00 p.m.
當然可以，太太，不過恐怕今天洗衣太晚了，我們可以明天下午 4 點前送回來。

16. Could you leave your laundry on the _____, if you are going out, sir?
如果您要外出，先生，請您把送洗的衣服放在床上好嗎？

17. I'd like this garment _____, please.
我想把這件衣服干洗一下。

18. We don't have the _____ and we cannot take responsibility for any damage.
我們沒有這方面的設施，而且我們對任何損壞不負責任。

19. Do you have a _____ service for clothes?
你們有織補衣服服務嗎？

20. There is a _____ on this jacket, I'd like it removed before it's dry-cleaned.
這件夾克上有污跡，我想在干洗前先去掉它。

21. I spilled some _____ on it.
我把醬汁灑在上面了。

22. We will do our best to remove the stain but we cannot _____ the result.
我們將盡力去掉這塊污跡，但我們不能保證肯定可以去掉。

23. We deliver your laundry within 4 hours at 50% _____ charge.
我們在 4 小時之內將衣服送給您，並加收 50% 費用。

24. We will _____ the cost of the laundry and the new sweater.
我們將退還您洗衣服的費用和毛衣錢。

25. We are very sorry for the _____.
給您帶來不便，非常抱歉。

26. I'm in a hurry, I have to _____ it tomorrow morning.
這件衣服要快件，明天早上我要穿。

27. The _____ of this woolen sweater isn't clean, please ask them to re-wash it.
這件羊毛衫領口沒洗乾淨，請再洗一遍。

28. Sorry, the cuff of your shirt was _____ when we pressed it. We'll pay for it.
對不起，這件襯衫的袖子燙壞了，我們會賠您的。

29. Please fill out this pressing _____ and I will call the laundry to get it for you.
請填寫這張燙衣表格，我會叫洗衣服務來收取的。

30. I have two _____ of trousers and some other things to be washed and ironed.
這兩條褲子要洗，還有一些要燙。

31. Here is the money we found in the _____ of your pants.
這是我們在您交洗的褲子口袋裡發現的錢。

32. This coat is not mine, and there is one shirt _____.
這件衣服不是我的，我還缺一件襯衣。

33. There is a _____ missing on my coat, can you sew on a new one for me?
我掉了一個扣子，你能幫我配一個嗎？

34. Your laundry is here, sir. Please _____ it.
先生，您的衣服拿來了，請您核對一下。

II. Make a dialogue according to the following situation.（創作情景對話）

客人 B 電話到客房部，想瞭解洗衣服務時間。然後客房部告訴客人早上十點前送，當天下午四點可以把衣服洗好送到房間內。如果是下午三點送洗，第二天中午前可以把衣服送回房間。價目表在抽屜裡。然後客人 B 讓服務員來房間取一下衣服。服務員說 5 分鐘就去取衣服。請根據以上情景，創作一篇不少於 100 個單詞的英文對話。

Unit 5　Emergencies　突發事件

Background（背景知識）

All hotels are required by law to provide their guests with a list of specific emergency procedures. Because one of the most common emergency situation in a hotel is a fire, emergency procedures typically include a detailed map of the floor the room is on and an outline of the route to the closest exit. Emergency preparedness also includes a list of what to do once you've evacuated the hotel as well as what to do in the event that you're prevented from evacuating.

Hotels often post a room-specific evacuation map on the back of the door to each room. The nearest exit is marked, as are all other exits on the floor in case the closest one is blocked. Hotels that don't put individualized maps in each room are required by law to provide general floor plan maps. Front desk staff may highlight the nearest stairwells and exits to a guestroom on a paper copy.

Emergency evacuation procedures begin by moving to exit when an alarm sounds, even if you suspect it's a drill. Before opening the door, you should feel it for heat and look for smoke coming underneath the door. Barring any smoke or flames, hotel procedures dictate that you should exit via the safest, shortest route possible. If there's heavy smoke, you should stay low to the ground. Never use elevators during an emergency evacuation; they may become stuck mid-descent, or the shaft may fill with smoke. Also, the fire department may need to use the elevators to assist immobile people.

Situational dialogues（情景對話）

Dialogue 1

H—Housekeeping   G—Guest

H: Housekeeping. May I help you?

G: Yes, I'm Steve Garrett in Room 523. I've lost my camera.

H: I'm sorry to hear that, sir. Shall we check your room for you?

G: No, I've already checked there.

H: Could you describe your camera in detail? I'll keep a record.

G: Yes, of course. It's a black Canon AE.

H: When and where did you first find your camera missing, Mr. Garrett?

G: This morning after I came back to my room.

H: Where did you go?

G: I had breakfast in the coffee shop. Then I went to the Drug Store and straight back to my room.

H: We will check there with the security section, too. When will you be checking out, Mr. Garrett?

G: Tomorrow morning.

H: We'll do our best to find your camera in the shortest possible time.

G: Thank you.

Chapter Two Housekeeping 客房部

(About eight hours later.)

H: Good evening. Housekeeping. May I speak to Mr. Garrett, please?

G: Speaking.

H: We have found your camera.

G: Wonderful! Thanks a lot. Where was it?

H: It was in the Drug Store. Could you come to our office on the first floor?

G: Great! Housekeeping Department on the first floor.

H: That's right, sir.

Translation（譯文）

H——客房服務員　G——客人

H：客房部。請問需要幫忙嗎？

G：是的，我是523房間的史蒂夫·加勒特。我找不到相機了。

H：聽到這個消息我很難過，先生。我們檢查一下您的房間好嗎？

G：不用，我已經檢查過了。

H：您能詳細描述一下你的相機嗎？我做個記錄。

G：好的。這是一個黑色的佳能 AE。

H：您第一次是在什麼時間、什麼地點發現相機不見了，加勒特先生？

G：今天早上，我回到房間時。

H：您去哪兒了？

G：我在咖啡廳吃早餐。然後去了藥店，又直接回房間。

H：我們會和保安部到那兒查看一下。您什麼時候退房，加勒特先生？

G：明天早上。

H：我們會盡力在最短的時間內找到您的相機。

G：謝謝你。

（約八小時後。）

H：晚上好。客房部。我找加勒特先生。

G：我就是。

H：我們已經找到了您的相機。

G：太好了！非常感謝。在哪裡找到呢？

H：在藥店。您能來一樓我們的辦公室一下嗎？

G：太好了！一樓客房部。

H：對的，先生。

Words and expressions（單詞和短語）

emergency 突發事件

housekeeping 客房部

camera 照相機

check 查找

describe 描述

detail 細節

record 記錄

drug store 藥店，雜貨店

straight 直接地

describe sth. in detail 詳細地某物

keep a record 做記錄

security section：保安部

in theshortest possible time 在盡可能短的時間內

Dialogue 2

R—Room Attendant　F—Female guest　M—Male guest

R：Housekeeping. May I help you?

F：Yes. Could you please come here? My husband slipped in the bathroom. One of his legs is bleeding.

R：Don't worry, Madam. Your name and room number, please?

F：It's Nelson in Room 1905. Please hurry.

(Five minutes later, the attendant arrives.)

R：Leave it to me, Madam. Mr. Nelson, can you try to stand up?

M：Yeah… oh it hurts.

R：Slowly. I will help you to your bed.

M：Thanks. The floor was too slippery when I stepped out of the tub.

R：I see. I'll send up someone to clean the bathroom later. Now I need to clean your wound and dress it.

M：OK.

R：Mrs. Nelson, could you please press here to stop the bleeding?

F：Sure.

R：The bleeding will stop soon. I will call the doctor right now.

F：Thank you very much. You've been very helpful.

R：My pleasure.

Translation（譯文）

R——客房服務員　F——太太　M——先生。

R：客房部。需要幫忙嗎?

F：是的。請你過來一下好嗎？我丈夫在浴室滑倒了。一條腿在流血。

R：別擔心，夫人。請告訴我您的姓名和房號？

F：1905 房間的納爾遜。請快點。

(五分鐘後，服務員到達。)

R：交給我吧，夫人。納爾遜文先生，你能設法站起來嗎？

M：嗯……噢，好痛啊。

R：慢點。我扶您到床上去。

M：謝謝。我走出浴缸時，地板太滑了。

R：我明白。我晚點再派人打掃浴室。現在我需要清理、包紮您的傷口。

M：好的。

R：納爾遜夫人，您可以按壓這裡止血嗎？

F：好的。

R：血很快就會止住。現在我馬上打電話給醫生。

F：非常感謝。你幫了大忙了。

R：不客氣。

Words and expressions（單詞和短語）

husband 丈夫

slip 滑

bleed 流血

hurry 快點

leave it to me

hurt 感到疼痛

slippery 滑的

tub 浴缸

wound 傷口

dress 包紮

press 按壓

right now 馬上

Dialogue 3

R—Room Attendant   G—Guest

R：I'm sorry to hear that you are not feeling well. What's the matter, Mr. Raphael?

G：I didn't sleep well last night. I'm feeling a little dizzy now.

R: Shall I call a doctor for you?

G: Not necessary. Do you have some penicillin pills? I'll pay you.

R: Sorry, Mr. Raphael. I can't buy you the medicine. It's against the hotel's regulations. Let me accompany you to the hotel clinic.

(After seeing the doctor)

R: Well, may I turn on the heating switch above the minibar. You may take the medicine with the water.

G: Ok.

R: Don't worry, sir. You will be all right soon. Are you feeling better now?

G: Yes. That's very kind of you.

R: My pleasure.

Translation（譯文）

R——客房服務員　G——客人

R：聽到您不舒服我很難過。拉斐爾先生，您怎麼了？

G：我昨晚沒睡好。現在感覺有點頭暈。

R：我幫您叫一個醫生好嗎？

G：不必了。你有青黴素片嗎？我會付錢給你。

R：對不起，拉斐爾先生。我不能給您買藥，這是違反酒店規章制度的。讓我陪您去酒店診所吧。

（看過醫生後）

R：嗯，我可以打開小冰箱上的加熱開關嗎。您可以用水服藥。

G：好的。

R：別擔心，先生。您很快就會好的。現在感覺好些了嗎？

G：是的。你太好了。

R：不客氣。

Words and expressions（單詞和短語）

dizzy 頭暈

necessary 必要的

penicillin 青黴素

pill 藥丸

medicine 藥物

against 違反

accompany 伴隨

clinic 診所

switch 開關

pleasure 愉快

Dialogue 4

A—Hotel operator   B—Guest

A：Hotel operator. How can I assist you?

B：Can you call the police for me? My daughter is missing. I can't find her anywhere.

A：Please don't panic, Madam. Where is the last time you saw your daughter?

B：I took her to breakfast an hour ago. I told her to wait for me when I went to the washroom, but when I came back, she's gone.

A：How old is your daughter? Did anyone notice where she went?

B：She's seven and she wears a blue dress. The waitress said she went to the washroom as well, but I didn't see her.

A：Don't worry, Madam. Your daughter might still be in the hotel. I will contact the Security Department. They will help you find her.

B：Thank you very much.

Translation（譯文）

A——接線員   B——客人

A：酒店接線員。請問需要幫助嗎？

B：你能幫我報警嗎？我的女兒走丟了。我到處都找不到她。

A：請不要恐慌，夫人。您最後看到您女兒是在什麼地方？

B：一小時前我帶她去吃早餐。我去洗手間，讓她等我。但是當我回來的時候，她不見了。

A：您女兒多大了？有人注意到她去哪裡了嗎？

B：她7歲了，穿一條藍色的裙子。服務員說，她也去了洗手間，但我沒有看到她。

A：別擔心，夫人。您的女兒可能還在酒店裡。我會聯繫保安部。他們會幫您找到她。

B：非常感謝。

Words and expressions（單詞和短語）

operator 接線員

assist 協助

police 警察

daughter 女兒

panic 恐慌

washroom 廁所

notice 留意到

wear 穿著

waitress 女服務員

as well 也

contact 聯繫

Exercises（練習題）

I. Complete the sentences.（補全句子）

1. When and _____ did you last see it?
您最後一次見到它是在什麼時候、什麼地點？

2. I'm sorry to _____ that.
我對此深表遺憾。

3. ShallI _____ the police for you, sir?
我為您報警好嗎，先生？

4. I'll call the _____.
我去叫救護車。

5. The hotel is on _____.
酒店失火了。

6. A _____ is coming.
臺風要來了。

7. Take the emergency _____!
走緊急出口！

8. Hope you'll _____ soon.
希望您早日康復。

9. Will you please come to our _____ on the first floor?
請您到一樓我們的辦公室來一趟好嗎？

10. You need to sign your name on the Lost and Found Form. And _____ to take your ID card along.
您需要在失物招領單上簽字，記著帶上身分證。

11. Please remain _____; we have informed the Engineering Dept. for rush repair.
請保持冷靜，我們已經通知工程部來搶修了。）

12. I'll send someone from the Maintenance Department to your room. But I'm afraid you'll have to pay for the _____.
我馬上從維修部派人到您的房間去，但恐怕您得賠償損失。

II. *Make a dialogue according to the following situation.* （創作情景對話）

酒店發生劫持時間，員工 B 報警，警察讓員工保持冷靜，觀察匪徒的面貌、身型、衣著、髮型等特徵。請根據以上情景，創作一篇不少於 100 個單詞的英文對話。

Unit 6　Other Housekeeping Service　客房其他服務

Background（背景知識）

The housekeeping department as a whole is required to make the guests' stay comfortable and pleasing. Any reasonable request must be fulfilled. Whenever and wherever possible, the staff should offer to do extra things for the guests. What is more, whenever there is an opportunity to sell the services, the staff should take it and persuade the guests to use the hotel services as possible. They should make sure that they are really selling what the guests wants to buy.

Situational dialogues（情景對話）

Dialogue 1

C—Clerk　G—Guest

C：Housekeeping. May I help you?

G：Yes. Do you have a converter? I want to use my hairdryer, but it's 315 V.

C：I am sorry. Another guest is using it right now. Can you wait for another 15 minutes?

G：15 minutes? I can't wait that long. I will have a party half an hour later. You have only one converter?

C：We have two, but the other one is broken. Oh, Madam, a guest has returned the hairdryer. We can lend it to you now.

G：Wonderful. This is Mrs. Robert in room 2413.

C：Mrs. Robert, the attendant will be up in three minutes.

Translation（譯文）

C——職員　G——客人

C：客房部。請問有什麼需要幫忙嗎？

G：是的。你們有變壓器嗎？我想用我的吹風機，但它是 315 伏的。

C：我很抱歉。另一個客人現在使用。您能等 15 分鐘嗎？

G：15 分鐘？我不能等那麼久。半小時後我有一個聚會。你們只有一個變壓器嗎？

C：有兩個，但另一個壞了。哦，夫人，客人歸還了吹風機。現在可以把它借給您了。

G：太好了。我是2413房間的羅伯特夫人。

C：羅伯特夫人,服務員將在三分鐘後送到。

Words and expressions（單詞和短語）

converter 變壓器

hairdryer 吹風機

broken 壞的

lend 借出

Dialogue 2

S—Staffmember　G—Guest

S：Room center. MayI help you?

G：Yes, please. I am Carmela Sean, Room 1816. My husband and I are going to a party this evening. I'd like to know if you could take care of my little son Olaf. It's only till midnight.

S：I see. Madam. But the attendants are not allowed to look after children while they're on duty.

G：What should I do then?

S：Don't worry, ma'am. We have very good baby-sitting service in the hotel. All the baby-sitters are experienced and reliable.

G：Oh! That's great!

S：The baby-sitting service charges RMB 50 per hour, with a minimum of two hours.

G：It sounds reasonable.

S：For how many hours do you need the service?

G：Well, we'll have to leave at 8：00 p.m. and won't return until midnight.

S：Ok, that'll be about 4 hours. The housekeeper will go to your room and check through the details with you. Then you sign up a confirmation form.

G：Thank you for your help.

S：We are always at your service.

Translation（譯文）

S——職員　G——客人

S：這裡是房務中心。請問需要幫助嗎?

G：是的,麻煩你了。我是1816房間的卡米拉·肖恩。我和丈夫今晚要參加一個聚會。請問你們能否照看我的小兒子奧拉夫。只到午夜就行。

S：我明白了,夫人。但是服務員上班時間不允許照顧孩子。

G：那我應該怎麼辦呢?

S：別擔心，夫人。我們酒店有很好的保姆服務。所有的保姆都經驗豐富，值得信賴的。

G：哦！太好了！

S：保姆服務費每小時50元，最少兩個小時起價。

G：聽起來很合理。

S：您需要多少小時的服務呢？

G：嗯，我們晚上8點出門，午夜返回。

S：好的，這大概要4個小時。客房服務員會去您的房間，跟您對接詳細事宜。然後請您在表單上簽字確認。

G：謝謝你的幫助。

S：隨時為您服務。

Words and expressions（單詞和短語）

take care of 照看

midnight 午夜

look after 照料

on duty 當班、值班

baby-sitting service 看護嬰幼兒服務

baby-sitters 看顧小孩的人

experienced 經驗豐富的

reliable 可靠的

minimum 最少的，最低的

reasonable 合理的

check through 仔細檢查

confirmation form 確認單

Dialogue 3

H—Housekeeper G—Guest

H：Good afternoon, sir. May I help you?

G：Yes. I am the guest of room 662. I left my key card in my room.

H：Do you have any identification, sir?

G：I'm afraid not. I didn't bring my wallet. I came out for lunch.

H：Do you remember your visa number or something else that can prove your identity? Otherwise we can't open the door for you.

G：Yes, I understand. I remember my passport number. It's CN30J28P8.

H: Mr. William, right? Wait a minute, sir. The attendant will arrive with the spare key card.

G: Thanks.

Translation（譯文）

H——客房服務員　G——客人

H：下午好，先生。需要幫忙嗎？

G：是的。我是662房間的客人。我把鑰匙卡落在房間裡了。

H：先生，您有什麼身分證明嗎？

G：恐怕沒有。我沒有帶錢包。我是出來吃午餐的。

H：您還記得您的簽證號碼或其他可以證明您身分的信息嗎？否則我們不能為您開門。

G：是的，我理解。我記得護照號碼。CN30J28P8。

H：威廉先生，對嗎？請等一下，先生。服務員會拿備用鑰匙卡上來。

G：謝謝。

Words and expressions（單詞和短語）

identification 身分證明

wallet 錢包

lunch 午餐

prove 證明

identity 身分

otherwise 否則

Dialogue 4

C—Clerk　G—Guest

C: Good evening, housekeeping. What can I do for you?

G: Good evening. There seems to be something wrong with the radiator. It's so cold here.

C: Your room number, sir?

G: It is 443.

C: I see. I'll immediately notify the maintenance department to deal with it.

G: Thank you.

(Five minutes later)

C: Maintenance. May I come in?

G: Come in, please.

C: The radiator is not operating right.

G: Yes, it's too cold. I can't sleep.

C: I am sorry for that, sir. Let me check it. (After a while) I am sorry sir. The radiator is beyond repair for now. I am afraid you have to use the air conditioner, or you can call the front desk and change to another room.

G: Well, I guess I can do with the air conditioner.

Translation（譯文）

C：晚上好，這裡是客房部。需要幫忙嗎？

G：晚上好。散熱器好像有問題。這裡太冷了。

C：先生，您的房間號碼是多少？

G：443。

C：我明白了。我立即通知維修部來解決。

G：謝謝你。

（五分鐘後）

C：維修員。我可以進來嗎？

G：請進。

C：散熱器運轉不正常。

G：是的，太冷了。我無法睡覺。

C：我很抱歉，先生。讓我檢查一下。（過了一會）對不起，先生。散熱器眼下是無法修理的。恐怕你必須使用空調，或者你可以打電話給前臺，換到另一個房間。

G：嗯，我用空調吧。

Words and expressions（單詞和短語）

radiator 暖氣片

immediately 立即

notify 通知

maintenance 維修

operate 運轉

beyond 超過

repair 修理

air conditioner 空調機

Exercises（練習題）

I. Complete the sentences.（補全句子）

1. It is the time you would like to be _____ up.

您要求被叫醒的時間到了。

2. We have a _____ wake-up service.

我們有電腦叫醒服務。

3. I'll have them brought for you as _____ as possible.

我會馬上讓人替您購買。

4. All the baby-sitters are well-educated and _____.

這些保姆都受過良好的教育，並且很有經驗。

5. Sorry we have no such flowers, but I can buy it in the flower _____ nearby.

對不起，這種鮮花飯店沒有，但我可以幫您到附近的花店購買。

6. We'll send someone to _____ it immediately.

我們會馬上派人來修的。

7. Some part needs to be _____. I will be back soon.

有個零件要換了。我片刻就來。

8. I'm afraid we don't offer any shoe-cleaning service, but you may find the shoeshine paper in the _____.

恐怕我們不提供擦鞋服務。不過，您在床頭櫃那可以找到擦鞋紙。

9. I'm terribly sorry, sir. It takes time to repair. I'm afraid you have to change to _____ room.

先生，非常抱歉。修理需要時間，恐怕您得換個房間了。

10. We have arranged a room on the 16th floor for you. And the bellman will help you with your _____.

我們在16樓給您安排樓另一個房間。行李員會幫您將行李拿過去的。

11. I'll send for an _____ from the maintenance department.

我馬上從維修部派電工到您房間去。

12. We can have it _____. Please wait a few minutes, madam.

我們會把電視機修好的。夫人，請您稍等幾分鐘。

II. Make a dialogue according to the following situation.（創作情景對話）

客人提出叫醒服務要求時，一定要記錄客人姓名、房號、叫醒時間，並切記實施。然後通知下一班的總機員工，保障第二天要按時叫醒服務。請根據以上情景，創作一篇不少於100個單詞的英文對話。

Chapter Three　　Food and Beverage 餐飲部

Unit 1　　Reservation　　預訂餐臺

Background（背景知識）

Hotel departments work together everyday, each relying on the other to do their part in delivering a product they all can be proud of, each interacting with each other.

The Food and Beverage Department is a major factor in hotel operation, it offers the guests good food and drinks besides comfortable rooms and other conveniences, mainly covering the restaurant, banquet, grill room, bar, coffee shop, cafeteria, room service and lounge service. The mission and goal of this department is to offer high quality service to the guests and meanwhile win lots of new and return guests.

The Food and Beverage Department involves many people working together as a team. So group cohesiveness is particularly important. It is useful for all hotel employees to be familiar with their hotel's Food and Beverage operation, so that they will be able to notify guests of what is available at the hotel. Some hotels regularly invite staff to dine at the various sections of this department in order to ensure that they remain familiar with offerings, specialties, hours of operation etc.

Reservations usually have the first contact with the most guests before they actually arrive. Since most restaurant reservations are made by the telephone, telephone procedures are the most important in the reservation section. This is the guests'first impression of the hotel and incorrect handling will often result in a loss of business. So it is of great importance that the employees are pleasant, courteous, friendly and helpful at all time.

Situational dialogues（情景對話）

Dialogue 1

R—Reservationist　　G—Guest

R: Good afternoon, Shunxing Restaurant. How may I help you?

G: I'd like to reserve a table for dinner this evening, please.

R: Certainly, sir. For how many people, please?

G: Three of my friends, around 8:00 p.m.

R: Yes sir. Would you like a table in the main restaurant or in a private room?

G: A private room, please.

R: Certainly, sir. We'll have Rose Hall reserved for you, will that be fine? May I have your name and cell phone number, please?

G: Sure, it's Andy, and my cell phone number is 13113141314.

R: Mr. Andy, 13113141314, thank you. By the way, we will reserve the private room till 9:00 p.m.

G: OK, I see.

R: I'd like to confirm your reservation: Mr. Andy for 3 persons, at Rose Hall around 8:00 p.m. this evening; your cell phone number is 13113141314.

G: That's right, thank you.

R: We look forward to serving you, Mr. Andy. Thank you for calling.

Translation（譯文）

R——預訂員　G——客人

R：下午好，順興川菜。能為您效勞嗎？

G：我想預定今天晚上的餐位。

R：好的，先生，請問有幾位？

G：三位，大約下午八點左右。

R：我明白了。您想訂在大廳還是包房呢？

G：包房吧。

R：好的，先生。我們為您預留玫瑰廳，好嗎？能留下您的姓名和電話號碼嗎？

G：當然，我叫安迪，手機是13113141314。

R：安迪先生，13113141314。順便說一下，您預定的包房會保留到晚上九點。

G：好的，我知道了。

R：我想跟您確認一下您的預訂：安迪先生，預訂今晚的玫瑰廳，到達時間是 晚上八點，手機是13113141314。

G：是的，謝謝。

R：我們恭候您的光臨，安迪先生。謝謝您的來電。

Words and expressions（單詞和短語）

around 大約

main 主要的

restaurant 餐廳

private room 包廂

cell phone 手機

look forward to 期待

Dialogue 2

Situation：A guest is asking to arrange a welcome banquet. 客人要求安排歡迎宴會

A—Waiter　B—Guest

A：Good morning. East Sea Fishing Village. May I help you?

B：Hello. This is Jason Stone from the APL Corporation. We'd like to have a welcome banquet in your restaurant. Can you arrange it for us?

A：Certainly, Mr. Stone. When would you like your banquet?

B：At 7：30 tomorrow evening.

A：How many people will there be in your party?

B：There will be 58 altogether.

A：Then I'll arrange six tables for you. Could I recommend the Rose Hall? It's newly decorated, and it's well equipped and spacious. I'm sure you'll like it.

B：That sounds good. We'll take it.

A：Then how much would you like to spend for each table?

B：At about 2,000 yuan and we'd like the typical Cantonese dishes.

A：That's fine. Would you like to order when you come?

B：Yes. And please prepare some Great Wall dry wine, Tsing Tao Beer, champagne coconut milk and pineapple juice.

A：All right. What kinds of fruits would you like to have?

B：Grapes, tangerines, mangos and pineapples.

A：OK. So let me repeat what you've told me：a welcome banquet in the Rose Hall at 7：30 tomorrow evening; six tables for fifty-eight people at 2,000 yuan a table; Cantonese dishes; drinks and fruits. Is that correct, Mr. Stone?

B：Yes. That's correct.

A：Thank you. Mr. Stone. We'll make sure everything is ready for you. I hope you'll enjoy it.

B：Thank you very much. Good Bye!

Translation（譯文）

A——服務員　B——客人

A：早上好，東海漁村酒樓，您需要幫助嗎？

B：你好。我是 APL 公司的杰森·斯通。我們想在貴酒樓舉行一個歡迎宴會。你能安排一下嗎？

A：當然可以，斯通先生。請問宴會什麼時候舉行？

B：明天晚上 7 點 30 分。

A：請問一共有多少人？

B：總共 58 人。

A：那我替您安排 6 張餐桌吧。安排在玫瑰廳怎麼樣？這個廳剛剛裝修過，設備先進，也很寬敞。您一定喜歡。

B：聽起來不錯。就要這間吧。

A：請問每桌的標準是多少？

B：每桌 2,000 元左右，要正宗的粵菜。

A：好的。你們來了之後點菜嗎？

B：是的。請給我們準備一些長城干白葡萄酒、青島啤酒、香檳酒、椰子汁和菠蘿汁。

A：好的。您想要些什麼水果呢？

B：葡萄、橘子、芒果和菠蘿。

A：好的。我重複一下您說的需求：歡迎宴會明天晚上 7 點 30 分在玫瑰廳舉行；6 張餐桌共 58 人；每桌 2,000 元的標準；正宗粵菜；另有酒水和水果。對嗎，斯通先生？

B：非常正確。

A：謝謝您，斯通先生。我們會為您準備妥當的，希望你們喜歡。

B：非常感謝。再見!

Words and expressions（單詞和短語）

welcome banquet 歡迎宴會

altogether 總共

recommend 推薦

well equipped 裝飾精美

spacious 寬敞

typical 典型的

Cantonese 廣東的

prepare 準備

wine 葡萄酒

champagne 香檳酒

coconut 椰子

pineapple 鳳梨

juice 果汁

fruit 水果

grape 葡萄

tangerine 橘子

mango 芒果

repeat 復述

Dialogue 3

R—Reservationist   G—Guest

R：Good afternoon. Friendship Restaurant. May I help you?

G：Yes, I'd like to reserve a table for four at 8：00 this evening.

R：Just a moment, sir. Let me check and see if there is vacancy at the restaurant.

G：OK.

R：I'm sorry, sir. There aren't any tables left for 8：00 this evening.

G：I would appreciate it, if it could be arranged.

R：I'll try my best. We can give you one at 9：00.

G：No, it's too late.

R：I'm sorry, sir.

G：That's all right.

R：We look forward to having you with us next time, sir. Thank you for calling.

G：Goodbye.

R：Goodbye, and have a nice day!

Translation（譯文）

R——預訂員   G——客人

R：下午好。友誼餐廳。可以為您效勞嗎?

G：是的，我想預定一個今晚八點的四人桌。

R：請稍等，先生。我查一下，看看是否有空位。

G：好的。

R：對不起，先生。今晚8點沒有任何空位了。

G：如果可以安排，我會非常感激。

R：我會盡力的。9點我們可以給您安排一桌。

G：不用了，太晚了。

R：對不起，先生。

G：沒關係。

R：我們期待您下次光臨，先生。謝謝您的來電。

G：再見。

R：再見，祝您愉快！

Words and expressions（單詞和短語）

friendship 友誼

vacancy 空位，空桌子

appreciate 感謝

arrange 安排

appreciate 感激

Exercises（練習題）

I. Translate the following sentences into Chinese.（把下列句子譯成中文）

1. For what time, sir?

2. When would you like your table?

3. How many people are there in your party?

4. Who's the reservation for?

5. May I have your name, please?

6. Thank you for calling us.

7. I'm sorry, sir. All the tables are reserved until 7：00 p.m. What about a table for 8：00 p.m.?

8. The only tables available are for after 8：00 p.m.

9. Is there any place you would prefer to sit?

10. We look forward to having you with us.

11. We will make all the arrangement.

II. Translate the following sentences into English.（把下列句子譯成英文）

1. 我需要預約位子嗎？

2. 我想要預約3個人的位子。

3. 我們共有6個人。

4. 我們大約在8點到達。

5. 我要如何才能到達餐廳？

6. 我想要預約今晚7點2個人的位子。

7. 我很抱歉。今晚的客人相當多。

8. 我們大概需要等多久？

9. 9點應該沒問題。

10. 今天的推薦餐是什麼？

11. 我們想要面對花園的位子。

12. 餐廳是否有任何服裝上的規定？

13. 女士是否需著正式服裝？

14. 請不要穿牛仔褲。

III. Make a dialogue according to the following situation.（創作情景對話）

現在是下午4點，服務員A接到一個訂餐電話，客人詢問了餐廳晚餐營業時間，並提出預定一張明晚晚餐的桌子，A查看了預訂簿確認明晚還可以預定後詢問了客人的姓名、電話、用餐人數以及是否還有其他要求等，客人回答其叫David，電話號碼13878990021，共兩人用餐，希望能夠預定靠窗的餐桌。服務員A重複客人的預約情況進一步確認。請根據以上情景，創作一篇不少於100個單詞的英文對話。

Unit 2　Receiving Guests　迎客服務

Background（背景知識）

The management and operation of food and beverage departments has been described as the most technical and complex in the hotel-keeping and catering trade. One main responsibility of this department is to receive guests.

The job of the hostess is to welcome and seat the guests when they arrive, and to arrange reservations in restaurants. In many cases, the hostess also takes drink orders from the guests after they have been seated. She also thanks the guests when they leave.

Waiters and waitresses also play an important role in the operation, because they have more contact with the guests than other restaurant employees. They must be attentive to the needs of the guests, and they can explain items on the menu that are unfamiliar to the guests or make recommendations about dishes.

Situational dialogues（情景對話）

Dialogue 1

A—Attendant　G—Guest

A：Good evening, sir. Welcome to Chunxing Restaurant. Do you have a reservation?

G：Yes, I have.

A: May I have your name and room number, please?

G: Andy, my room number is 4212.

A: Yes, sir, you have reserved a table for four people, non-smoking area. This way, please.

Translation （譯文）

A——服務員　G——客人

A: 晚上好，先生。歡迎光臨春興餐館。請問您有預訂嗎？

G: 有的。

A: 先生，請問您貴姓？您的房號是多少？

G: 我是4212的房客，安迪。

A: 好的，先生。有您的預定，四個人，無菸區。這邊請。

Words and expressions （單詞和短語）

non-smoking 無菸的

this way 這邊走

Dialogue 2

A: Good evening, sir. Welcome to Shunxing Restaurant. Dinner for how many people, please?

G: A table for four, please.

A: Yes, sir. This way, please. How about the table by the window?

G: Fine. Thanks.

A: This way, please.

Translation （譯文）

A: 晚上好，先生。歡迎光臨順興餐館。請問有幾位用餐呢？

G: 要個4人桌。

A: 好的，先生，那張靠窗的桌子怎麼樣？

G: 好，謝謝你。

A: 這邊請。

Words and expressions （單詞和短語）

A table for four 四人桌

Dialogue 3

A: Good evening, Sir. Our tables are full now; would you mind waiting for a while or would you prefer another restaurant?

G：I would like to wait.

(2 minutes later)

A：I'm sorry to have kept you waiting. Here is a table available. This way please.

G：It doesn't matter. Thank you.

A：You are welcome.

Translation（譯文）

A：晚上好，先生。我們的餐廳現在已經客滿了，您想換一家餐廳嗎？

G：我再等一下好了。

(兩分鐘後)

A：很抱歉讓您久等了，這邊有空位，請這邊走。

G：沒關係，謝謝你。

A：不客氣。

Words and expressions（單詞和短語）

full 滿的

available 空的

matter 有關係

Dialogue 4

H—Hostess   G—Guest   L—Lounge bartender

H：Good evening, madam, sir. Welcome to our restaurant. Have you made a reservation?

G：I'm afraid not.

H：A table for two?

G：For four, please. My friends are coming in a few minutes.

H：I'm sorry to say that we haven't got any vacant table at present. Would you please wait in the lounge for about 10 minutes? I'll seat you when a table is ready.

G：All right.

L：What would you like to drink, madam and sir?

G：Two sherry on the rocks.

L：Just a moment, please.

(10 minutes later.)

H：I'm sorry to have kept you waiting, madam and sir. Now we have a table for you. Come this way, please.

G：Good.

H：Will this table be all right?

G: Very nice.

H: Sit down, please. Here's the menu. I'll come back in a few minutes to take your order.

Translation（譯文）

H——女主人　G——客人　L——休息室酒吧招待

H：晚上好，夫人，先生。歡迎光臨本餐廳。請問您預訂了嗎？

G：恐怕沒有。

H：一張兩人桌嗎？

G：四人桌。我的朋友們幾分鐘後到。

H：很抱歉，目前我們沒有任何空桌。請在休息室等候大約10分鐘好嗎？一有空桌我就請你們入座。

G：好的。

L：你們想喝點什麼，夫人，先生？

G：兩杯雪利，加冰塊。

L：請稍等。

（十分鐘後）。

H：對不起，讓你們久等了。現在有一個空桌給你們了。請這邊走。

G：好的。

H：這張桌子可以嗎？

G：非常好。

H：請坐。這是菜單。我一會兒再回來為你們點單。

Words and expressions（單詞和短語）

lounge 休息室

bartender 酒吧招待員

vacant 空的，未被占用的

seat 為……提供座位

Sherry 雪利酒（在飯前或與開胃品同時享用的開胃酒之一）

on the rocks 加冰

menu 菜單

return 返回

vacant 空缺的

lounge 休息室

care to 願意

Dialogue 5

H—Hostess   G—Guest

H: Good evening, sir. Welcome to our restaurant. Do you have a reservation?

G: Yes, you will find the reservation under Jones.

H: Wait a minute, please. Yes, Mr. Jones. We are expecting you. You have reserved a private room for six people, right?

G: Yes.

H: Would you come this way please? It's on the third floor.

G: Thank you very much.

H: You are welcome. Here it is. Is this room all right?

G: Yes, quite good.

H: I am glad you like it. Please take your seat, and help yourself with some fruits. I will make a cup of tea for you.

G: Thanks. May I have the menu?

H: Sure. Would you like to order now?

G: No. I just want to have a look. There are still five of us coming.

H: I see. I will come back later. Is there anything else you need?

G: Oh, yeah. If anyone looks for me, please bring him here.

H: Certainly, sir.

Translation（譯文）

H——女咨客　G——客人

H：晚上好，先生。歡迎光臨本餐廳。請問您有預訂嗎？

G：是的，以瓊斯的名義預訂的。

H：請等一下。是的，瓊斯先生。我們正在恭候您。您預訂了一間6人包廂，對吧？

G：是的。

H：請這邊走好嗎？在三樓。

G：非常感謝。

H：不客氣。到了。這間可以嗎？

G：是的，很好。

H：很高興您喜歡。請您入座，並享用一些水果。我給您上一杯茶。

G：謝謝。可以給我菜單嗎？

H：好的。你要點菜了嗎？

G：不。我只是想看看。我們還有五個人要來。

H：我明白了。我稍後回來。您還有什麼需要嗎？

G：哦，是的。如果有人找我，請把他領到這裡。

G：當然可以，先生。

Words and expressions（單詞和短語）

expect 恭候

look for 尋找

private room 包廂

help yourself with 隨便吃

floor 樓層

Exercises（練習題）

I. Translate the following sentences into Chinese.（把下列句子譯成中文）

1. Good evening, sir. Welcome to our restaurant. Do you have a reservation?

2. This way, please.

3. A table for two?

4. I'm sorry to say that we haven't got any tables available at the moment?

5. I'm sorry, that table is already reserved.

6. Would you please wait a few minutes in the lounge over there? I'll let you know as soon as the table is ready.

7. Please take your seats. Here's the menu. I'll be back in a few minutes to take your order.

II. Translate the following sentences into English.（把下列句子譯成英文）

1. 您的桌子已準備好。

2. 請問您有早餐券嗎？

3. 很抱歉，現在沒有空桌子。

4. 你們是否願意與那位女士共用一張桌子。

5. 我幫你們換一張靠角落的桌子。

6. 很抱歉，那張桌子已被預定了。

7. 如果您明天或哪天需要的話，我可以幫您預定。

III. Make a dialogue according to the following situation.（創作情景對話）

客人 B 前往餐廳用餐，服務員 A 在餐廳門側迎接，A 向 B 問好後詢問是否有預定餐位，客人 B 回答沒有預定，服務員 A 進一步詢問客人用餐人數以及對於餐位的要求，客人 B 回答共四人用餐，希望餐位相對安靜。服務 A 提出推薦餐位並引領入座。請根據以上情景，創作一篇不少於 100 個單詞的英文對話。

Chapter Three　Food and Beverage 餐飲部

Unit 3　Western Food　西餐服務

Background（背景知識）

Western-style food refers to the food or dinner cooked according to the customs of western countries. Western-style food is originated in Europe and the European cooking methods were conveyed by Marco Polo to China. Later, after the Opium War, it was transferred from「residential dish」to「western restaurant」and then「western-style food restaurant」run by Chinese people. It was only served for some officials and businessmen at that time.

In recent years, the number of foreign guests increased rapidly. More and more hotels have western food services. At the same time, more and more Chinese people have accustomed to the hobby of eating western food.

Over the past ten years, western food has become more diversified and has increasingly provided Chinese consumers with unconventional enjoyment, a complete turn from traditional Chinese food culture. China now has western-style cuisine of various nationalities and special characteristics. French, German and Italian restaurants are the most popular. Western-style fast food is led by McDonald's and KFC; bars, coffee shops, Japanese sushi bars, South Korean cuisine and south-east Asian delicacies are also ascendant.

Situational dialogues（情景對話）

Dialogue 1

W—Waiter　G—Guest

W: Good afternoon, sir and madam. May I take your order now?

G: Yes. We will have two sirloin steaks. Medium well, the same as usual.

W: Two sirloins, medium well. How about some desserts or soups?

G: What kinds of desserts do you serve?

W: We have chocolate pie, tiramisu, tart and all kinds of fruit cakes.

G: I will have chocolate pie. And a strawberry cake for my wife.

W: Certainly. would you care for some wine?

G: No. thanks. Just juice will do.

Translation（譯文）

W——服務員　G——客人

W：下午好，先生，女士。我可以為你們點菜了嗎？
G：是的。我們要兩份沙朗牛排。七分熟，像往常一樣。
W：兩份沙朗牛排，七分熟。來一些甜點或湯怎麼樣？
G：你們有什麼甜點？
W：我們有巧克力派，提拉米蘇，蛋撻和各種各樣的水果蛋糕。
G：我要巧克力派。再來一個草莓蛋糕給我的太太。
W：好的。您需要來點酒嗎？
G：不，謝謝。只要果汁就可以了。

Words and expressions（單詞和短語）

western food 西餐

sirloin steak 西冷牛排

medium well 七分熟

dessert 甜食

soup 湯

serve 招待

chocolate pie 巧克力餡餅

tiramisu 提拉米蘇

tart 蛋撻

strawberry 草莓

care for 喜歡

Dialogue 2

W—Waitress   G—Guest

G：Is it time for breakfast?

W：Yes. We serve breakfast from 7 to 9 in the morning. What kind of breakfast do you want to have, continental or American?

G：We would like to have the continental breakfast. It will save some time.

W：And what kinds of fruit juice would you like to have? we have a variety of them: pineapple, orange, grapefruit.

G：But do you serve hot coffee?

W：Certainly. What coffee do you prefer, white or black?

G：A cup of white coffee and the pineapple juice, please.

W：And the meal?

G：We would like two pieces of bread.

W: Buttered or not?

G: No butter.

W: OK. One moment, please.

Translation（譯文）

W——服務員　G——客人

G：現在是早餐時間嗎？

W：是的。我們從早上 7 點到 9 點供應早餐。您想要哪種早餐，歐陸式還是美式？

G：我們想要歐陸式。能省點時間。

W：您需要哪種果汁？我們有多種選擇：菠蘿汁、橙汁、柚子汁。

G：但是你們有熱咖啡嗎？

W：當然有的。您喜歡什麼樣的咖啡，加奶還是清咖啡？

G：請給我來一杯加奶咖啡，一杯菠蘿汁。

W：需要什麼餐食呢？

G：我們想來兩片麵包。

W：配黃油嗎？

G：不要黃油。

W：好的。請稍等。

Words and expressions（單詞和短語）

continental breakfast 歐陸式早餐

a variety of 多種多樣的

grapefruit 柚子

prefer 更喜歡

butter 黃油

Dialogue 3

W—Waitress　G—Guest

W: Here's your poached fillet of fish with cheese, sir.

G: Oh, I'm afraid there is a mistake. I think what I ordered was not this one.

W: Sorry, sir. I've just had a check and I found this was exactly what you had ordered.

G: Is that so? But I don't like it. Can I have a change?

W: Well, poached fillet of fish with cheese is our house specialty and very popular with our guests with a strong and pleasant flavor. It's worth a try.

G: All right. I'll try it. One more thing, I've ordered another dish, sirloin steak. Can it be served sooner? It's been quite a long time since I ordered it.

W: I'm terribly sorry, sir. It takes a long time to prepare the sirloin steak and there are many guests today as well. Please wait for some more time and I'm going to the kitchen to tell the chef to hurry. I believe the dish will be ready soon.

G: Thank you. It is very kind of you.

W: My pleasure.

Translation（譯文）

W——服務員　G——客人

W：這是您點的芝士焗魚，先生。

G：哦，恐怕搞錯了。我想我點的不是這個菜。

W：對不起，先生。我剛查過了，這正是您點的。

G：是嗎？但我不喜歡。能換嗎？

W：哦，芝士焗魚是本店的特色菜。味道很好，很受客人喜愛，值得一試。

G：好的，我試試看。還有，我已點了另一道菜，沙朗牛排。能早些上嗎？我已經下單很久了。

W：非常抱歉，先生。沙朗牛排需要很長時間來烹飪，而今天客人又很多。請再等一會兒，我會去廚房讓廚師快點做。我相信很快就好了。

G：謝謝你。你太好了。

W：不客氣。

Words and expressions（單詞和短語）

poached fillet of fish with cheese：芝士焗魚（fillet 指里脊，柳肉，魚片）

mistake 錯誤

exactly 確切地

house specialty 本店特色菜

popular 受歡迎的

strong 濃鬱的

pleasant 令人愉快的

flavor 味道，風味

worth 值……的

chef 廚師

hurry 加快

Dialogue 4

W—waiter　G—guest

W: Sorry to disturb you, sir and madam. Here are your drinks and appetizers: smoked salmon and tuna salad.

G：Wonderful. We are starving.

W：Here is T-bone steak. Where shall I put it?

G：There. It's hers.

W：And the sirlon steak must be yours, sir.

G：That's right. Thank you.

W：You have also ordered one cream of mushroom soup and one coffee cheesecake. May I serve the soup to you now?

G：Later, please.

(20 minutes later)

W：Here is your soup.

G：Oh, I was just thinking about it. Thank you.

W：You are welcome. The soup is hot. Please be careful. Shall I serve your cake now or later?

G：Serve it now, please.

W：Your coffee cheesecake. May I take away the plate?

G：Yes.

W：Leave it to me, sir. Enjoy your meal.

Translation（譯文）

W——服務員　G——客人

W：對不起，打擾一下，先生，女士。這是你們的飲料和開胃菜：熏鮭魚和金槍魚沙拉。

G：太好了。我們真的餓了。

W：這是T骨牛排。把它放在哪裡？

G：那邊吧，是她點的。

W：西冷牛排一定是您的，先生。

G：是的，謝謝你。

W：你們還點了一份奶油蘑菇湯，一個咖啡芝士蛋糕。請問現在就要端上來嗎？

G：請稍後。

(20分鐘後)

W：這是您的湯。

G：哦，我正好想起它。謝謝你。

W：不客氣。湯是熱的，請小心。您的蛋糕現在上還是稍後上？

G：請現在上吧。

W：您的咖啡芝士蛋糕。我可以拿走盤子嗎？

G：好的。

W：先生，讓我來，祝你們用餐愉快。

Words and expressions（單詞和短語）

disturb 打擾

appetizer 開胃菜

smoked salmon 熏鮭魚

tuna 金槍魚

salad 沙拉

starve 餓死

T-bone steak T骨牛排

cream 奶油

mushroom 蘑菇

cheesecake 酪餅

plate 盤子

Exercises（練習題）

I. Translate the following sentences into Chinese.（把下列句子譯成中文）

1. Do you have vegetarian dishes?

2. Do you have a menu in Chinese?

3. Would you like something to drink before dinner?

4. What kind of drinks do you have for an aperitif?

5. May I see the wine list?

6. May I order a glass of wine?

7. What kind of wine do you have?

8. I'd like to have some local wine.

9. I'd like to have French red wine.

10. Could you recommend some good wine?

11. May I order, please?

12. What is the specialty of the house?

13. Do you have today's special?

14. Can I have the same dish as that?

15. I'd like appetizers and meat (fish) dish.

16. I'm on a diet.

17. I have to avoid food containing fat (salt/sugar).

Chapter Three　Food and Beverage　餐飲部

II. Translate the following sentences into English.（把下列句子譯成英文）

1. 現在可以為您點菜了嗎？
2. 您要喝點什麼？
3. 您的牛排要全熟的、半熟的，還是三分熟的？
4. 您的雞蛋怎麼吃？
5. 您要不要試試我們的招牌菜，麻婆豆腐？
6. 您還要點什麼？
7. 您點的東西很快就會準備好。
8. 這是您的菜肴。
9. 請慢用，先生。
10. 您的咖啡是先上還是餐後上呢？

III. Make a dialogue according to the following situation.（創作情景對話）

客人 B 前往西餐廳用餐，服務員 A 引領其入座後將菜單遞給 B 點單，B 點了一瓶法國雷歐登干紅並詢問有什麼推薦菜品，A 詢問 B 是否有忌口，B 回答沒有忌口的，但希望能夠相對清淡些。於是 A 向 B 推薦頭盤可考慮魚子醬，魚子醬主要是由明太魚魚子跟蝦醬製作而成，湯品推薦匈牙利時蔬牛肉湯，主菜可考慮安格斯西冷，蛋白質含量高，而且脂肪含量較低。於是 B 點了一份魚子醬、一份匈牙利時蔬牛肉湯、一份香煎朦朧魚、一份安格斯西冷外加一份巧克力布朗尼藍莓汁配香草冰淇淋，A 詢問 B 安格斯西冷是需要幾分熟，B 回答七分熟，A 重複 B 所點菜品進一步確認並說明大概需要等候十分鐘左右。請根據以上情景，創作一篇不少於 100 個單詞的英文對話。

Unit 4　Chinese Food　中餐服務

Background（背景知識）

China covers a large territory and has many nationalities, hence a variety of Chinese food with different but fantastic and mouthwatering flavor. Since China's local dishes have their own typical characteristics, generally, Chinese food can be roughly divided into eight regional cuisines, which has been widely accepted around. They are Shandong cuisine, Canton cuisine, Sichuan cuisine, Anhui cuisine, Fujian cuisine, Jiangsu cuisine, Zhejiang cuisine and Hunan cuisine. Certainly, there are many other local cuisines, which are famous, such as Beijing Cuisine and Shanghai Cuisine.

Chinese cooking has a history which is much longer than that of French cuisine. It uses almost all of the meat, poultry, fish and vegetables including foodstuffs which may appear rare or even distasteful to the foreigners.

Marco Polo once said about Chinese food.「They eat all sorts of meat including that of dogs and other animals of every kind.」Talking about the eating habits of Cantonese, people often say humorously that they make use of anything with four legs except tables.

Situational dialogues（情景對話）

Dialogue 1

W—Waiter　G—Guest

W: Good evening, sir. Are you ready to order now?

G: Yes. Since this is our first visit to China, I'd like to try some Chinese food today. Could you please give us some advice?

W: Of course, sir. Chinese food can be divided into eight big cuisines, such as Canton food, Sichuan food, Beijing food, etc.

G: Is there any difference?

W: Yes, Guangdong food is a bit light. It uses various kinds of seafood. Sichuan food is spicy and hot. It stresses the use of seasonings. Beijing food is heavy and spicy.

G: Could you tell me some famous specialties about these cuisines.

W: Canton food is famous for its roast suckling pig. Beijing food is especially famous for its roast Beijing duck.

G: How about Sichuan food?

W: I think Mapo beancurd and shredded meat in chili sauce are quite special.

G: Very good. I prefer seafood. I'd like to try Canton food.

W: Now, would you please look over the menu first, sir? The Canton dishes are listed on the right. Please take your time. I'll be back in a few minutes to take your order.

G: All right.

Translation（譯文）

W——服務員　G——客人

W：晚上好，先生，您準備點菜了嗎？

G：是的。這是我們第一次來中國，所以今天我想嘗嘗中國菜。你能給我們一些建議嗎？

W：當然可以，先生。中國菜分為八大菜系，如廣東菜，四川菜，北京菜，等等。

G：有什麼區別嗎？

W：是的，廣東菜清淡一些。它採用各種海鮮作為食材。四川菜麻辣濃香，強調調料

的使用。北京菜則味重香濃。

G：你能介紹一些關於這些菜系的著名特色菜肴嗎？

W：廣東菜以烤乳豬聞名。北京菜以北京烤鴨特別出名。

G：四川菜怎麼樣？

W：我覺得麻婆豆腐和魚香肉絲很特別。

G：非常好。我偏愛海鮮，想吃廣東菜。

W：現在請您先翻看菜單，好嗎，先生？廣東菜列在右邊。請慢慢看。我一會兒就回來為您點菜。

G：好的。

Words and expressions（單詞和短語）

Chinese food 中餐

since 由於

advice 建議

be divided into 劃分為

cuisine 烹飪，菜系

such as 例如

etc. <拉>及其他，等等

light 清淡的

various 各種各樣的

seafood 海鮮

spicy 香辣的

hot 辣的

stress 強調

seasoning 調味

heavy 口味重的

famous 著名的

specialty 特色菜

roast suckling pig 烤乳豬

roast Beijing duck 北京烤鴨

beancurd. 豆腐

shred 切成條狀

chili 紅辣椒

sauce 醬汁

look over 過目

take your time 別著急，慢慢來

Dialogue 2

W—Waiter　G—Guest

W：Here is your hot towel, sir.

G：Fine, thanks.

W：May I take your orders now?

G：Certainly. Do you have steamed grouper?

W：Sorry, I'm afraid we're sold out of grouper.

G：Then I'll have sliced duck with mushroom soup, steamed whole crabs and egg drop soup with minced beef, one for each.

W：Sorry, sir. You've ordered two soups, one is sliced duck soup and the other is the minced beef soup. May I suggest changing one?

G：That's a good idea. Change the duck soup for crisp chicken skin slices.

W：I'm terribly sorry, but this dish has to be ordered in advance before meals. How about sweet and sour pork?

G：How do you prepare it?

W：Actually it's fried pork in pieces. It tastes sweet and sour and is rather tasty. Want to have a try?

G：It sounds good. All right, I'll try it.

Translation（譯文）

W——服務員　G——客人

W：先生，這是您的熱毛巾。

G：好，謝謝。

W：我現在可以為您點菜了嗎?

G：當然。你們有清蒸石斑魚嗎?

W：對不起，石斑魚恐怕賣完了。

G：那我要北菇燴鴨絲，清蒸螃蟹與牛肉碎蛋花湯，每樣一份。

W：對不起，先生。您點了兩個湯，一個是鴨絲湯，另一個是牛肉碎湯。我建議換一個，好嗎?

G：好主意。把鴨絲湯換成片皮炸雞吧?

W：非常抱歉，這道菜必須在餐前提前預訂。您看咕嚕肉怎麼樣?

G：這道菜怎麼做呢?

W：實際上是炒豬肉。味道酸甜，很好吃。您想要嘗嘗嗎?

G：聽起來不錯。好吧，我試試。

Words and expressions（單詞和短語）

towel 毛巾

steam 蒸

slice 薄片

crab 蟹，蟹肉

mince 切碎

beef 牛肉

crisp 脆的

in advance 預先

sour 酸的

pork 豬肉

fried 煎的

steamed grouper：清蒸石斑魚

sliced duck with mushroom soup：北菇燴鴨絲

minced beef：牛肉碎

crisp chicken skin slices：片皮炸雞

sweet and sour pork.：咕嚕肉

Dialogue 3

W—Waiter　G—Guest

W：Good morning, gentlemen. How many teas would you like to order?

G：Three, please.

W：Very good, sir. We serve black tea, green tea, Oolong tea and Pu'er tea. Which kind of tea do you prefer?

G：I want black tea and both of them would like Pu'er tea.

W：Yes, sir. And we have various kinds of sweet and salty dim sum served on the dim sum trolley, and different types of congee are also available. You can choose what you like.

G：What are these, please?

W：Those are spring roll with shredded chicken, stuffed bun with meat, steamed dumpling with stuffing, noodle soup with shrimps.

G：Please give me two of this and one of that.

W：All right. Here is your breakfast, gentlemen.

Translation（譯文）

W——服務員　G——客人

W：早上好，先生們。你們需要幾杯茶呢？

G：請來三杯吧。

W：好的，先生。我們有紅茶、綠茶、烏龍茶和普洱茶。你們喜歡哪一種？

G：我想喝紅茶，他們想喝普洱茶。

W：好的，先生。手推車上有各種甜味和咸味點心，也有不同種類的粥品。你們可以根據自己喜好挑選。

G：這是什麼呢？

W：這些是雞絲春卷，肉包子，蒸餡餃，蝦仁湯面。

G：請給我拿兩份這個，一份那個。

W：好的。這是你們的早餐，先生們。

Words and expressions（單詞和短語）

black tea 紅茶

Oolong tea 烏龍茶

Pu'er tea 普洱茶

dim sum 點心

trolley 手推車

congee 粥

spring roll 春卷

bun 小圓麵包

dumpling 包子，餃子、湯團

shrimp 蝦

Dialogue 4

W—Waiter　G—Guest

W: Sorry to have kept you waiting. Here's your Beijing roast duck, sir.

G: Aha, it looks good, but I don't know how to eat it. There're so many plates.

W: I will show you, sir. This one is duck skin which is crispy and tasty. These two are duck meat.

G: Oh, I see. And what is that pancake for? I don't think I ordered it.

W: The pancake is served along with the duck. You can wrap the skin and the meat together in the pancake, along with the Chinese onions and sauce here.

G: I will have a try. Hum! It's great. I like it. What is the sauce made from? I have never tasted it before.

W: It is called sweet bean sauce which is made from wheat flour, sugar, salt and fermented soy beans. It is very popular with Chinese people.

G: I can see why. Thank you very much.

W: You are welcome. Enjoy your meal.

Translation（譯文）

W——服務員　G——客人

W：對不起，讓您久等了。先生，這是您點的北京烤鴨。

G：啊哈，看起來不錯，但是我不知道怎麼吃。有好多盤子。

W：我教您，先生。這是鴨皮，又脆又好吃。這兩個是鴨肉。

G：哦，我明白了。那個煎餅是做什麼用的呢？我沒有點這道菜呢。

W：煎餅是搭配鴨肉的材料。您可以用煎餅把皮和肉一起包裹起來，在這蘸上大葱和醬料。

G：我來試試。哦！太棒了。我喜歡。醬料是用什麼做的？我從來沒有嘗過。

W：那是甜豆醬，是由麵粉、糖、鹽和發酵的大豆做成的，是中國人很喜歡的調味料。

G：我知道原因了。非常感謝。

W：不客氣。祝您用餐愉快。

Words and expressions（單詞和短語）

pancake 薄煎餅

along with 連同……一起

wrap 裹，包

onion 洋葱

bean 豆

wheat 小麥

flour 麵粉

sugar 糖

salt 鹽

ferment 發酵

Exercises（練習題）

I. Translate the following sentences into Chinese.（把下列句子譯成中文）

1. We've got a set menu.

我們有套餐提供。

2. We have a buffet. You can have all you want.

我們提供自助餐,您可以選擇你們喜歡的食物。

3. I would like to recommend lemon duck to you.

我想向您推薦檸檬鴨。

4. The dish is rather delicious.

這道菜相當美味。

5. Why don't you try the chef's recommendation?

要不要試一試廚師長的推薦菜?

6. Is everything satisfactory?

一切都滿意吧?

7. Here's your bill. Please check it. You may sign the bill, and the hotel will charge you when you leave.

給您帳單。請查看一下。您可以簽單,酒店會在您離店時一起給您結帳。

II. Translate the following sentences into English.(把下列句子譯成英文)

1. 歡迎光臨我們餐館。您是來參加約翰先生婚宴的嘉賓嗎?

Welcome to our restaurant. Are you here for the wedding banquet of Mr. John?

2. 現在可以上菜了嗎?

May I serve the dishes now?

3. 希望您用餐愉快。

Please enjoy your meal.

4. 今天的特價菜是麻婆豆腐,6折優惠。

Today's special is Mapo Tofu with a 40% discount.

5. 您的這瓶葡萄酒已經斟完了,請問還需要一瓶?

This bottle of wine is finished. Would you like one more?

6. 您的菜需要分一下嗎?

May I separate the dish for you?

7. 您要不要來點烈性酒呢?要是喜歡酒精度低的話,我們這還有米酒。

Do you care for something a little stronger? If you prefer something milder, you may try some rice wine available here.

8. 先生,您對我們的飯菜還滿意嗎?

Are you satisfied with the meal, sir?

9. 打擾了,女士。我給您換一個骨碟好嗎?

Excuse me, madam. Shall I change a new side plate for you?

10. 三百人用餐的收費是15,000元,不含酒水飲料。

Chapter Three　Food and Beverage 餐飲部

The charge for a 300-person-dinner party is RMB 15,000 yuan, excluding beverages.

11. 對不起，我們餐廳14日晚餐的餐位已經訂滿了。

I am sorry, sir. Our restaurant is fully booked on the evening of 14th.

12. 餐食通常從左側服務，酒水通常從右側服務。

Food is usually served from the left and beverages are served from the right.

13. 訂餐有人均100元、150元和180元三種標準，您想要訂哪一種？

For set menus, the expenses per head range from RMB 100 yuan, RMB 150 yuan to RMB 180 yuan. Which would you prefer?

III. Make a dialogue according to the following situation. （創作情景對話）

客人B前往中餐廳用餐，服務員A引領其入座後將菜單遞給B點單，幾分鐘後A向前詢問是否需要點單及口味偏好，B回答更喜歡川菜，A幫B翻到川菜菜單頁，B詢問有沒有推薦菜，A問B有沒有忌口的，B回答不吃海鮮。於是A向B推薦了水煮牛肉、夫妻肺片以及麻婆豆腐，這三種菜都是川菜的代表菜品。B點了一份涼拌黃瓜、一杯金桔檸檬、一份水煮肉片、一份夫妻肺片、一份麻婆豆腐外加一份炒時蔬。A詢問當前季節時蔬主要有生菜跟空心菜，請問要哪一種？B回答要炒生菜。A重複B所點菜品進一步確認。請根據以上情景，創作一篇不少於100個單詞的英文對話。

Unit 5　At the Bar　酒吧服務

Background（背景知識）[①]

Bars are found in most luxury, commercial and medium-sized hotels, usually near the lobby and restaurant so that they are accessible to local patron as well as hotel guests. Besides snacks and a range of alcoholic and non-alcoholic beverages, there often is live music during specific hours. Prices range from moderate to expensive, in keeping with the markets that patronize the establishment and the level of service provided by the hotel.

Generally speaking, there are two kinds of lists available in a restaurant and a bar. One is the「drink list」and the other is called「wine list」. A wine list is only wine, but the drink list can include wine, spirits and non-alcoholic beverages. In other words, a drink list can have alcoholic and non-alcoholic drinks.

Pouring drinks is only one thing a bartender does. Good bartenders, like good chefs, have a

---

① 背景知識部分摘自網路，有改動。原文網址：https://work.chron.com/converse-bartender-19292.html

lot of responsibilities. The head bartender has to keep a record of the entire stock of beverages. He also supervises the training of his men and the cleanliness of the bars. Like chefs, bartenders know ingredients and measurements. They know when to shake and when to stir. They know the special glasses for all drinks and make sure there are always a supply of clean ones. They use good liquors if they want to keep a good clientele. Waiters and waitresses should be able to explain various drinks to their clients. They also try to boost the sale of drinks by suggesting cocktails before dinner, wines during dinner, and liqueurs after dinner.

The ability to converse with all types of customers in a relaxed and casual manner goes along way toward creating an inviting atmosphere that will bring people back. Learn how to strike up a conversation and keep yourself up on current events—especially sports. Be a good listener and try and keep the conversations light and friendly. Make certain your attention is evenly decided among all the patrons, but remember that some people in a bar do not want to socialize.

Situational dialogues（情景對話）

Dialogue 1

B—Bartender   G—Guest

B: Good evening, ladies and gentlemen. Do you have a reservation?

G: I am afraid not. We are just passing by.

B: I see. Do you want to sit by a table or by the bar?

G: Anywhere away from the band. It's too noisy.

B: Certainly, miss. Would you please come this way? what would you like for a drink?

G: I will have mango shake and two bottles of Yanjing beer for them. We still have three of us coming.

B: Very well, miss. One mango shake and two bottles of Yanjing. I will be back in a minute.

Translation（譯文）

B——酒吧服務員   G——客人

B：晚上好，女士們，先生們。請問你們有預訂嗎？

G：恐怕沒有，我們是碰巧路過。

B：是這樣啊。你們想坐在餐桌邊，還是吧臺邊？

G：哪兒都行，離樂隊遠點就好，太吵啦。

B：好的，小姐。請這邊來。你們想喝點什麼？

G：我要芒果奶昔，他們要兩瓶燕京啤酒。我們還有三個人要來。

B：好的，小姐。一杯芒果奶昔，兩瓶燕京啤酒。我很快就回來。

G：謝謝。

Words and expressions（單詞和短語）

band 樂隊

noisy 喧鬧的

mango 芒果

shake 奶昔

Dialogue 2

B—Bartender　G—Guest

B：Good evening, sir. Bourbon on the rocks?

G：No. This time I'll try Chinese wine.

B：What about Mao Tai, one of the most famous liquors in China? It's rather strong, but never goes to the head.

G：Do people here drink a lot of liquors?

B：Some do, some don't. Many people in the north are fond of liquors. I think it has something to do with the climate.

G：Yes, it has. Some Mexicans are crazy. They drink a lot of liquors even in hot days. Are there any other famous Chinese liquors?

B：Yes, besides Mao Tai, we have Wu Liang Ye, Fen Jiu, Jian Nan Chun and so on.

G：They say that Shaoxing wine tastes quite good. What's it?

B：It's rice wine, a kind of still wine, somewhat like Japanese Sake. Shaoxing is a place in China.

G：I see.

B：By the way, we also have some good red wine and white wine, such as Zhangyu Red Wine, Great Wall White Wine and Dynasty Red Wine.

G：Thank you for telling me so much. I'll try them next time.

B：I'm always at your service.

Translation（譯文）

B——酒吧服務員　G——客人

B：晚上好，先生。加冰塊的波旁威士忌嗎？

G：不了。這一次我要嘗嘗中國葡萄酒。

B：茅臺行嗎？它是中國最著名的白酒之一。口感相當濃烈，但從來不上頭。

G：這裡的人們很愛喝白酒嗎？

B：有些人是的，有些不是。許多北方人喜歡白酒。我認為這與氣候有關。

G：是的。一些墨西哥人很瘋狂，他們甚至在炎熱的季節也喝很多白酒。還有其他中國著名白酒嗎？

B：是的，除了茅臺，我們還有五糧液、汾酒、劍南春，等等。

G：有人說，紹興黃酒口味不錯。它是什麼酒？

B：那是米酒，一種無氣泡酒，有點像日本的清酒。紹興是中國的一個地方。

G：我明白了。

B：順便說一下，我們也有一些好的紅酒和白葡萄酒，比如張裕紅酒、長城白葡萄酒和王朝紅酒。

G：謝謝你告訴我這麼多酒水知識。下次我會品嘗。

B：隨時為您服務。

Words and expressions（單詞和短語）

Bourbon 波本威士忌（美國產威士忌，由玉米發酵蒸餾而成，呈琥珀色）

on the rocks 加冰的

liquor 烈性酒

go to the head 上頭

are fond of 喜愛

have something to do with 與……有關

climate 氣候

Mexican 墨西哥的，墨西哥人

crazy 瘋狂的

besides 除了……之外，還有

somewhat 有些

liquor 烈酒

Sake （日本）清酒

Dialogue 3

W—Waiter　G1—Guest 1　G2—Guest 2　G3—Guest 3

W：What may I offer you?

G1：I don't know what I want. I'm not really a drinker.

W：An aperitif or some white wine?

G1：What do you suggest?

W：How about our special cocktail?

G1：That sounds good. How about you, Mary?

G2：I don't drink at all. Do you serve soft drinks?

Chapter Three Food and Beverage 餐飲部

W：Of course, madam. How about a non-alcoholic cocktail?

G2：It sounds interesting. I'll take that.

W：What would you like to drink, sir?

G3：Well, I'd like beer.

W：Any special brand, sir?

G3：What about your local brew? I hear it's good.

W：Yes, it's really worth a try. Then bottled or draught?

G3：We'll try the draught.

W：Fine. One special cocktail and one non-alcoholic cocktail for the ladies and one local beer. Would you like to have some snacks with your wine?

G2：Certainly, we would like to get some fresh supply.

W：Wait a moment, please. Your order will be ready right away.

Translation（譯文）

W——服務員　G1——客人1　G2——客人2　G3——客人3

W：你們需要喝點什麼？

G1：我不知道想喝什麼。我不太會喝酒。

W：開胃酒，或者一點白葡萄酒？

G1：你有什麼建議？

W：來點我們的特製雞尾酒怎麼樣？

G1：聽起來不錯。瑪麗，你呢？

G2：我壓根不喝酒。你們有軟飲料嗎？

W：當然有，夫人。不含酒精的雞尾酒怎麼樣？

G2：聽起來很有意思。我就要這個。

W：您想喝點什麼，先生？

G3：嗯，我想要啤酒。

W：要特定的品牌嗎，先生？

G3：當地的啤酒怎麼樣？我聽說不錯。

W：是的，真的值得一試。要瓶裝或是散裝？

G3：我們嘗嘗散裝的。

W：很好。女士們點了一杯特製雞尾酒和一杯不含酒精的雞尾酒，還有一杯本地的啤酒。你們需要一些小吃來配酒嗎？

G2：當然，我們想要一些新鮮的小吃。

W：請稍等。你們點的酒菜馬上就好。

Words and expressions（單詞和短語）

I'm not really a drinker. 我不大會喝酒。

aperitif 開胃酒

non-alcoholic cocktail 不含酒精的雞尾酒

brew 釀造的飲料

bottled 瓶裝的

draught 生啤酒、扎啤

snack 小吃

Dialogue 4

W—Waiter   G1—Male guest   G2—Female guest

W: Good evening, Mr. Will. And how are you, Madame?

G1: Good. Thanks. This is my wife

W: It is a pleasure to meet you, Mrs. will. What can I get you for a drink?

G1: Whiskey, as usual.

W: One whiskey on the rocks. And how about you, Madam?

G2: I don't know. I will have whiskey too.

W: How would you like your whiskey, straight or on the rocks?

G1: Straight, please.

W: Very well. Here is your drink Mr. will. And this is for you Mrs. Will.

G1: Thanks.

W: Did you enjoy yourselves in Beijing?

G1: Yes, we did. It's just a little bit tiring. The scenic spots are full of people.

W: Sorry to hear that. But if you would like to go somewhere quiet, I can recommend a few.

G1: Yes, please. we are leaving the day after tomorrow. and we would like to buy some souvenirs.

W: In that case, I suggest you go to the 798 Art Zone. It is quiet and relaxing. What's more, there are many artworks and beautiful little gifts for you to choose from.

G1: That's lovely. thank you.

Translation（譯文）

W——酒吧服務員   G1——男客   G2——女客

W：晚上好，威爾先生。您好，女士。

G1：很好，謝謝。這是我太太。

W：很榮幸見到您，威爾太太。您要喝點什麼？

G1：威士忌，老樣子。

W：一杯加冰威士忌。太太，您呢？

G2：不知道，我也要威士忌吧。

W：您要純的威士忌還是加冰塊？

G2：純的，謝謝。

W：好的，這是您的酒，威爾先生。這是您的，威爾太太。

G1：謝謝。

W：你們在北京過得開心嗎？

G1：是的，就是有點兒累，景點人都很多。

W：我很抱歉，但是如果你們想去安靜點的地方，我可以推薦幾個。

G1：好的，麻煩你了。我們後天就走，想買些紀念品回去。

W：那樣的話，我建議你們去798藝術工廠。那裡很輕鬆安靜，更重要的是那裡有很多藝術品和漂亮的小禮物，供你們選擇。

G1：那太好了，謝謝。

Words and expressions（單詞和短語）

straight 不加冰的

tiring 累人的

scenic spot 景點

somewhere 向某處

quiet 安靜的

recommend 推薦

souvenir 紀念品

relaxing 令人放鬆心情的

artwork 藝術品

Dialogue 5

W—Waitress　G1—Male guest　G2—Female guest

W：Good evening, sir and madam. Can I help you?

G1：Good evening. We'd like have some wine to drink. I want to look through the wine list first.

W：Yes sir. Here you are.

G1：I like a Spanish Cocktail. How about that?

W：It was mixed by Gin, soda water, lime juice and sugar.

G1：That's nice. How about you, my darling?

G2: I want to have non alcoholic cocktail. Do you have something to recommend?

W: Yes madam. I suggest you have a try of San Francisco Cocktail. It was mixed by pineapple juice, orange juice, grapefruit juice and soda.

G2: Sounds good. I'll take it.

W: OK. Please wait for a few minutes. They will be ready soon.

G1: All right.

Translation（譯文）

W——酒吧服務員　G1——男客　G2——女客

W：先生，女士，晚上好。有什麼需要幫忙嗎？

G1：晚上好。我們要喝點酒。我想先看看酒單。

W：好的，先生。給您。

G1：我喜歡西班牙雞尾酒。這個酒怎麼樣？

W：那是由金酒、蘇打水、酸橙汁和糖混合調制的。

G1：很好。你喝什麼，親愛的？

G2：我想喝不含酒精的雞尾酒。你有什麼推薦嗎？

W：好的，夫人。我建議您嘗嘗舊金山雞尾酒。它是由菠蘿汁、橙汁、柚子汁和蘇打水混合調制的。

G2：聽起來不錯，我就點這個。

W：好的。請等一會兒。你們的酒很快就上。

G1：好的。

Words and expressions（單詞和短語）

look through 瀏覽

wine list 酒水單

Spanish 西班牙的

cocktail 雞尾酒

gin 杜鬆子酒

soda 蘇打

lime juice 酸橙汁

nonalcoholic 不含酒精的

Exercises（練習題）

I. Translate the following sentences into Chinese.（把下列句子譯成中文）

1. What would like to drink?

2. Would you like something to drink before your meal, sir?

3. Your usual, sir?

4. With or without ice, please?

5. This wine is of the vintage of 1990.

6. Enjoy your drink, sir.

7. Would you like to try some Chinese alcohol?

8. Here is our wine list. We have a very extensive cellar.

9. The same again, sir?

10. The complimentary food would be on the house, of course.

II. Translate the following sentences into English.（把下列句子譯成英文）

1. 先生，對不起。這是我們的最低收費：兩杯飲料，每杯90元人民幣，再加10%的服務費。

2. 果汁杯怎麼樣？裡面有香檳酒、黑朗姆酒、橘子汁、檸檬汁、菠蘿汁、糖和姜啤。

3. 曼哈頓怎麼樣？這是一道經典雞尾酒：加拿大威士忌加苦艾酒和苦味酒。

4. 果味雞尾酒是由橘子汁、葡萄汁、西番蓮果汁、酸橙汁、芒果汁、菠蘿汁和一些獼猴桃糖漿調成的。

5. 我們這裡沒有生啤，只有瓶裝啤酒。

6. 夏威夷島衝浪與魔幻島相似，用椰子汁、菠蘿汁和橘汁沙冰調制而成。

7. 布朗先生，您今晚要喝點什麼？是不是像往常一樣來杯啤酒？

8. 這是普施咖啡，又叫彩虹酒。它是用幾種不同的餐後甜酒調制而成的，看上去像彩虹。

9. 論罐買啤酒比論杯買啤酒劃算。

10. 對不起，您喝醉了，我們不能賣酒給您。

III. Make a dialogue according to the following situation.（創作情景對話）

客人B前往酒吧吧臺就坐後，服務員A詢問是喝酒還是喝飲料，B回答一杯可樂，A詢問是常溫還是加冰還是加檸檬，B回答可樂少冰，外加一份薯條一份洋蔥圈。A重複B所點菜品進一步確認。請根據以上情景，創作一篇不少於100個單詞的英文對話。

Chapter Four　Conferences 會務部

Background（背景知識）

　　Meetings and conferences have become a major source of revenue for a large percentage of hotels. This revenue has generated primarily through the rental sleeping rooms, banquet, food and beverage, and meeting spacerental. Conference functions include greeting the guests and catering to their needs, organizing meetings, assisting in the set-up and breakdown of conferences and planning and servicing receptions, meals, dances, and any other event connected with a convention or independently sponsored banquet or function.

　　For a large-scale or an important banquet reservation, however, a face-to-face talk isnecessary. It is suggested a contract be concluded following the negotiation. Normally the following points must be specified in the contract: date and time, food covers, food price per cover, the set-up of the banquet venue and that of the tables, the name of the organizer, the liaison person, telephone number, way of payment and service charge.

　　Banqueting and conferences staff generally divides into two parts, one is in charge of sales, and the other is responsible for serving. Sales staff mainly includes banqueting and conference sales manager, banqueting and conference sales assistants. Serving staff involves banqueting and conference manager, banqueting headwaiters, banqueting captains and wine captains, banqueting waiters and wine waiters.

Situationaldialogues（情景對話）

Dialogue 1

S—Sales Manager　G—Guest

S：Good afternoon, business center. How can I help you?

G：Good afternoon. This is Mr. Russell from Room 425. I am organizing a business conference this Friday, so I'd like to know something about your meeting rooms.

S：Well, speaking of meeting rooms, we have small, medium, and large ones. How many attendees will there be?

G: About 300.

S: Then I think you will need a large room. A large meeting room can accommodate up to 450 people and charges 2,500 yuan half a day.

G: What about the facilities?

S: We provide audiovisuals including television, video recorder, and multimedia projector, etc. The use of facilities is free of charge.

G: I see. Please make sure to confirm my reservation.

Translation（譯文）

S——銷售經理　G——客人

S：下午好。這裡是商務中心，有什麼能為您效勞嗎？

G：下午好。我是425房間的拉塞爾先生。我這周五要組織一個商務會議，所以想瞭解一下你們的會議室。

S：哦，說到會議室，我們有小型、中型和大型會議室。請問你們有多少人出席會議呢？

G：大概三百人。

S：那我認為您需要一個大會議室。大會議室最多可容納四百五十人，每半天收費2500元.

G：設施情況呢？

S：我們提供視聽器材，包括電視機、錄像機、多媒體投影儀，等等。設施的使用是免費的。

G：我知道了，請您務必幫我預訂。

Words and expressions（單詞和短語）

business center 商務中心

conference（正式的）會議

attendee 出席者

accommodate 容納

facility 設施

audiovisual 視聽

multimedia 多媒體

projector 投影儀

video recorder 錄像機

free of charge 免費的

Dialogue 2

C—Clerk G—Guest

G: Good evening. I am Mr. Russell. I have reserved a large meeting room.

C: Yes, Mr. Russell. Good evening. If you don't mind, I will show you around the meeting room now.

G: I will appreciate that.

C: Here you are.

G: It is beautiful.

C: I am glad you like it. We have provided every guest with paper, pen and simultaneous interpretation conference system if you need it.

G: You are very considerate. But it is unnecessary, thanks.

C: The room is 30m in length, 18m in width and 7m in height. The French windows allow enough sunshine to come through. You can also enjoy a bird-view of the district through the window.

G: It is much better than my expectation.

C: Thank you. Do you have any special requirements for the room, such as mineral water, flowers, or microphone?

G: Yes. Please prepare a bottle of mineral water for every guest. Make it 310. Any brand will do.

C: What about flowers?

G: That will be unnecessary, but I'd like to use a lavalier microphone. Can you do that?

C: Sure, as you like.

Translation（譯文）

C——職員 G——客人

G：晚上好，我是拉塞爾先生。我預訂了一間大型會議室。

C：是的，拉塞爾先生，晚上好。如果您不介意的話，我現在帶您去看一下會議室。

G：太感謝了。

C：就是這兒。

G：太美啦。

C：很高興您能喜歡。我們為每位客人提供了紙筆，若您需要的話，還有同聲傳譯系統。

G：您很細心，但是不用了，謝謝。

C：這間會議室長30米，寬18米，高7米。落地窗保證陽光充足。您也可以從這裡一覽本地區的景色。

G：比我的預期好太多了。

C：謝謝。您對房間還有什麼特殊要求嗎？例如礦泉水，鮮花或者話筒等。

G：有的。請給每位客人準備一瓶礦泉水，一共310瓶吧，什麼牌子都行。

C：需要花嗎？

G：不用了，但是我想用領夾話筒，可以嗎？

C：當然可以。

Words and expressions（單詞和短語）

simultaneous interpretation 同聲傳譯

system 系統

considerate 考慮周到的

unnecessary 不必要的

length 長度

width 寬度

height 高度

sunshine 陽光

bird-view 俯瞰

district 地區

expectation 期望

mineral water 礦泉水

microphone 麥克風

brand 牌子

lavalier microphone 領夾話筒

Dialogue 3

S—Sales Manager G—Guest

S：Mr. Russell, I have been discussing dishes for the banquet with the manager of the Chinese restaurant this afternoon. Shall I brief you about the menu?

G：Yes, please.

S：We will prepare one bottle of Maotai and two bottles of Zhangyu cabernet for each table at the beginning.

G：All right.

S：15 dishes for every table, including three cold dishes, four dishes of seafood, two soups, five meat dishes and one sea cucumber soup for everyone on the table.

G：Lovely. What else?

S: We also provide a fruit plate of six kinds of fruits for each table at the end of the banquet.

G: I think that's quite enough.

S: I also suggest some flowers and plants here. What do you think?

G: That won't be necessary, but thank you. Well, I guess I have to pay a deposit for the banquet, right?

S: That's right, sir. That would be 82,890 yuan in total. You can pay half of it in advance.

G: No problem. I will pay by credit card.

Translation（譯文）

S——銷售經理　G——客人

S：拉塞爾先生，我今天中午和中餐廳的經理討論了一下宴會上的菜點。為您簡單通報一下菜單好嗎？

G：好的，請說。

S：我們先為每桌準備一瓶茅臺和兩瓶張裕解百納葡萄酒。

G：好的。

S：每桌十五道菜，包括三個涼菜，四道海鮮，兩個湯，五道肉菜，每人一份海參湯。

G：不錯呀，還有呢？

S：宴會的最後，我們會為每桌準備一份包含六種水果的果盤。

G：我想應該夠了。

S：我建議在這裡再擺放鮮花和植物，您覺得怎麼樣呢？

G：那就不用了，謝謝你。我需要支付定金，是嗎？

S：是的，先生，總計人民幣82,890元。您可以先付一半。

G：沒問題，我用信用卡支付。

Words and expressions（單詞和短語）

banquet 宴會

brief 簡要告知

cabernet 解百納葡萄酒

cucumber 黃瓜

fruit plate 果盤

deposit 押金，定金

in total 總共

in advance 預先

Dialogue 4

C—Clerk　G—Guest

C: Good morning, sir. Welcome to Telecommunication Products conference. Have you pre-registered?

G: Yes.

C: May I know your name, please?

G: My surname is Grayson.

C: Ok, Mr. Grayson. Let me check it up. I got it in the name list. Here is your meeting badge and meeting packet. Pencils and meeting paper are available on the desk. And you will find free refreshments at the bar in the lounge. May I show you to your seat?

G: That's good, thank you. By the way, where is the preparation area?

C: It's in the Jasmine Room on the right side of this multi-function room. I know you are about to give a speech, Mr. Grayson. It's my pleasure to lead you there to rehearse your audio-visual presentation.

G: Thank you very much.

C: It's my pleasure.

Translation（譯文）

C——職員　G——客人

C：早上好，先生。歡迎光臨電信產品發布會。請問您提前報名了嗎？

G：有的。

C：請問您貴姓？

G：我姓格雷森。

C：好的，格雷森先生。我來核對一下。您在名單裡。這是您的會議徽章和會議信息包。桌子上有鉛筆和會議用紙。您還可以在休息室的酒吧享用免費茶點。我帶您到座位好嗎？

G：那很好，謝謝你。順便問一下，準備區在哪裡？

C：在這間多功能廳右側的茉莉廳。格雷森先生，我知道您即將登臺演講。我帶您到那裡排練您的多媒體展示吧。

G：非常感謝。

C：不客氣。

Words and expressions（單詞和短語）

meeting badge 會議證章

meeting packet 會議資料袋

name sign 臺卡

keynoter 主要發言人

audio-visual presentation 多媒體發言

Dialogue 5

S—Conference Sales Manager   P—Conference Planner

P: Good afternoon, Ms. Tang. This is Jack Brown.

S: Good afternoon, Mr. Brown. It's my honor to receive your phone. Is there any further discussion about your conference?

P: Yes. What could you offer in the rooms?

S: We provide wireless Internet access to every room. You can also use our copiers, computers, fax machines or other amenities at certain prices.

P: That will be convenient. Fare enough. We can accept it.

S: Ok, Mr. Brown. Would you please come and sign a conference event order?

P: Sure. I will be in your office tomorrow.

S: Thank you so much. You can rest assured that we shall endeavor to make your conference a great success.

Translation（譯文）

S——會議銷售經理　P——會議策劃員

P：下午好，唐女士。我是杰克·布朗。

S：下午好，布朗先生。我很榮幸接到您的來電。您的會議還需要進一步的討論嗎？

P：是的。你們能在房間裡提供什麼設備？

S：我們提供互聯網接入，而商務套房和會議室則提供無線互聯網接入。您還可以付費使用本店的複印機，電腦，傳真機或其他設施。

P：那很方便。很合理。我們能接受。

S：好的，布朗先生。您能來簽一個會議活動訂單嗎？

P：好的。我明天會去你的辦公室。

S：非常感謝。您可以放心，我們會盡力使您的會議開得成功。

Words and expressions（單詞和短語）

conference affairs office 會務辦公室

wireless Internet access 無線網路接入

deposit 押金

conference event order 會議訂單

rest assured 確信無疑、放心

Dialogue 6

M—Conference Manager   H—Headwaiter

M: The meeting will start in one hour. It's an international tourism forum, which means a lot to our hotel, please make sure everything is arranged as required.

H: Yes. I've arranged routine cleaning early this morning, and I have checked the desk arrangement.

M: Remember to put one glass and a bottle of mineral water on each desk.

H: OK. I'll ask them to do it right now. Do you want me to check the facilities?

M: Yes, check the microphone and amplifier to see if they are in good condition. The speakers need to use the multimedia projector and laser pointer, so you must check the screen.

H: They are all ready.

M: Well done. The attendees will surely be satisfied with our preparation.

Translation（譯文）

M：會議經理　H：會議服務領班

M：會議將在一個小時後開始。這是一個國際旅遊論壇，對我們酒店意義重大，請確保一切安排符合要求。

H：是的。今天一大早我安排做常規清潔，還檢查了桌子的擺放。

M：記得在每個桌子上擺放一個玻璃杯和一瓶礦泉水。

H：好的。我現在馬上去交待他們。需要我檢查一下設施嗎？

M：要的，檢查麥克風和功放器，看看是否正常工作。發言人需要使用多媒體投影儀和激光指針，所以您必須檢查屏幕。

H：都準備好了。

M：干得不錯。與會者肯定會滿意我們的籌備工作。

Words and expressions（單詞和短語）

forum 論壇

routine cleaning 常規清潔

mineral water 礦泉水

pad 便箋紙

microphone and amplifier 麥克風和擴音器

multimedia projector 多媒體投影機

laser pointer 激光筆

Exercises（練習題）

I. Translate the following sentences into Chinese.（把下列句子譯成中文）

1. Can you give me some more details, please?

請您說得再具體一點,好嗎?

2. What size of conference do you plan?

請問多少人參加會議?

3. How many guests will there be, sir?

先生,請問將有多少客人出席呢?

4. What kind of function rooms do you need?

請問會議類型?

5. Is it a formal or informal event?

這個活動是正式的還是非正式的?

6. What time will you want the reception to start?

您希望招待會幾點開始呢?

7. Were you thinking of a full-day or a half-day function?

這個宴會您考慮是全天的還是半天的呢?

II. Translate the following sentences into English.（把下列句子譯成英文）

1. 這個宴會是在室內舉行,還是在室外舉行呢?

Will the banquet be an indoor or outdoor function?

2. 我會把我們各個宴會廳的詳細介紹寄給您。

I'll send you details of our various function rooms.

3. 您滿意我們的婚宴套餐嗎?

Would you like our set wedding lunch?

4. 需要我將我們的各個菜單傳真給您嗎?

Would you like me to fax you our range of menus?

5. 我將把人均費用情況和樓層平面圖一起寄給您。

I'll include details of prices per head and the floor plans.

6. 我們有好幾個大小不一的多功能廳。

We have several multifunctional rooms of various sizes.

7. 我們的荷花廳可容納300人。

Our Lotus Room can accommodate up to 300 people.

8. 我們可以提供無線話筒和袖珍話筒。

Wireless microphones and clip-on microphone are provided.

9. 我會在今天下班前把它傳真給您。

I'll fax it to you before the end of the day.

III. Make a dialogue according to the following situation. （創作情景對話）

餐廳服務員 B 接到客人預訂電話，客人說想要預訂 3 月 15 日晚上，包場用於舉辦生日宴，B 說需要查看預訂簿確認是否可以預訂，後跟客人說確認可以預訂，B 詢問客人的姓名、電話、總人數、會場需要布置什麼風格、菜品想要哪個套餐以及酒水是否自帶等，B 回答其叫 David，電話 18922334455，參加宴會總人數為 50 人左右，希望能夠布置成酒店官方網站上面宣傳的溫馨浪漫主題風格，菜品預訂 B 套餐，酒水自帶。B 詢問客人 3 月 15 日晚上大概幾點到達餐廳，幾點開席，是否還有其它安排，客人回答 3 月 15 日晚上六點左右到達餐廳，六點半左右開席，用餐最後會有生日歌環節可能需要一名餐廳服務員的幫助。B 重複一遍客人的預訂內容進一步確認信息。請根據以上情景，創作一篇不少於 100 個單詞的英文對話。

Chapter Five
Health & Recreation Service 康樂部

Unit 1 At the Recreation Center 健身中心

Background (背景知識)

For those with more of an energetic disposition, most of the premier hotels have an excellent fitness facilities available for the exclusive use of their guests. Of course, you don't have to exercise too hard, a swimming pool can be the best form of relaxation after a hard-day sightseeing. For daytime relaxation, the hotel health & recreation center has a gym, sauna and solarium. Most of the high-class hotel's health and recreational amenities are superior and complete with gymnasium, tennis court, swimming pool, snooker, mahjong, and sauna with massage center, a special night club, affords regular entertainment local or exotic. It is just like a city with its own night life.

Situational dialogues (情景對話)

Dialogue 1

R—Receptionist   G—Guest

R: Good morning, Health Club. What can I do for you?

G: Yes. This is Robert Giles from Room 1453. I heard the club here is excellent, so I'm calling to learn something about your service.

R: Very well, Mr. Giles. The Health Club is furnished with the latest sports equipment, such as treadmills, weight machines, chest press machines and so on.

G: Eh-huh.

R: And all professional fitness instructors will provide you with personal exercise plan.

G: That's interesting. Where is the club, please?

R: At the corner of the third floor. The club is open from 7 AM till midnight. You can come here at your convenience.

G: I see. Thank you.

Translation（譯文）

R——接待員　G——客人

R：早上好，健身俱樂部，我能為您效勞嗎？

G：是的，我是1453房的羅伯特·賈爾斯。我聽說這裡的俱樂部很棒，所以我想瞭解一下你們的服務。

R：好的，賈爾斯先生。健身俱樂部配有最新的運動器材，例如跑步機，舉重器，推胸器，等等。

G：嗯。

R：所有的專業健身教練還會為您制定個性化的健身計劃。

G：挺有意思。俱樂部位置在哪兒？

R：在三樓的轉角處，我們的營業時間是從早上7點到晚12點，歡迎您光臨。

G：明白了，謝謝。

Words and expressions（單詞和短語）

excellent 極好的；優秀的

furnish 裝備

equipment 裝備

treadmill 跑步機

Weight machine 舉重器

professional 職業的

fitness 健身

instructor 教練

personal 私人的

corner 角落

convenience 方便

Dialogue 2

C—Clerk　G—Guest

G: Excuse me. Are you a coach?

C: Yes. How can I assist you?

G: It is the machine. The buttons confuse me.

C: It is alright, sir. I will show you how the treadmill works.

G: Thank you.

C: Press the green button to start the machine, and the red button to stop it.

G: Ok.

C: This is the manual model which allows you to select your own choices of pattern and speed. You can have a try first. Not too hard at the beginning.

G: I see. And what is this?

C: That button is for speeding up, and the one next to it is for slowing down.

G: Oh, I got it.

C: You can also try the Fitness Test function here, which can measure your heart beats and other factors.

G: I will try that later. thank you.

Translation（譯文）

C——職員　G——客人

G：你好，請問你是教練嗎？

C：是的，需要幫忙嗎？

G：是關於這個機器的問題。我搞不懂上面的按鈕。

C：沒關係，先生。我來教您使用跑步機。

G：多謝。

C：按下綠色按鈕是啓動機器，紅色是停止。

G：好的。

C：這是手動模式，可以讓您選擇自己喜歡的模式和速度。您可以先試一下，開始的時候別太難。

G：我知道了。這個呢？

C：這個是加速用的。旁邊那個是減速用的。

G：哦，我明白了。

C：您也可以試一下健康測試功能。它能檢測您的心跳以及其他指標。

G：我一會兒再試，謝謝了。

Words and expressions（單詞和短語）

coach 教練

assist 幫助

button 按鈕

confuse 弄糊塗

manual 手動的

model 模式

select 選擇

pattern 式樣，款式

speed 速度

function 功能

measure 測量

factor 因素，指標

Dialogue 3

R—Receptionist　G—Guest

R：Good afternoon. Welcome to our hotel's swimming pool, sir. Can I help you?

G：I'd like to go swimming, but I am wondering how do you charge for it.

R：It's complimentary for the registered guests.

G：Oh, can you tell me what the depth is?

R：Certainly, sir. The deepest place is 2.5 meters and the shallow area is only one-meter in depth.

G：Where should I keep my belongings?

R：We have the separate locker room over there, and you can use them free of charge. And you can have a shower there.

G：By the way, do you sell swimming trunks here? I didn't bring mine.

R：Yes, you can find them at the shop beside the swimming pool.

G：Can you give me the key to the locker?

R：Yes, here you are.

G：Thank you.

R：Have fun. If you need anything, please tell me.

G：Thanks a lot.

Translation（譯文）

R——接待員　G——客人

R：下午好。歡迎光臨我們酒店的游泳池，先生。需要幫忙嗎？

G：我想去游泳，但是我不知道你們怎麼收費。

R：對入住的客人是免費的。

G：哦，能問一下水有多深嗎？

R：當然可以，先生。最深的地方是2.5米，淺水區深度只有1米。

G：我的物品怎麼保管呢？

R：我們在那邊有單獨的寄存室，您可以免費使用。您也可以在那裡淋浴。

G：順便問一下，你們這裡賣泳褲嗎？我沒有帶。

R：是的，您可以在游泳池邊的商店買到。

G：你能給我儲物櫃的鑰匙嗎？

R：好的，給您。

G：謝謝你。

R：遊得開心。如果有什麽需要，請告訴我。

G：非常感謝。

Words and expressions（單詞和短語）

complimentary 免費贈送的

separate locker room 獨立的更衣室

swimming trunks 游泳褲 / swimsuit 女士泳衣

hygienic 衛生的

every other day 每隔一天

warm up 熱身

Exercises（練習題）

I. Translate the following sentences into Chinese.（把下列句子譯成中文）

1. You can have a dip in our heated swimming pool. Swimming is one of the best ways to improve your health and keep-fit.

2. We have a well-equipped keep-fit gymnasium with all the latest recreational sports apparatus-exercise bicycles, weights, wall bars-that sort of thing.

3. Please wipe off the machines after use.

4. You can borrow a life buoy and use the separate locker room free of charge.

5. Do you need some help using that machine?

II. Translate the following sentences into English.（把下列句子譯成英文）

1. 您多久運動一次？

2. 加把勁。跟著我再做 5 次。

3. 這項運動能讓您的肩膀更有型。

4. 如果您覺得體力耗盡了，最好就停住。

5. 如果您拉傷肌肉或傷了背部，之後幾周都沒法運動了。

6. 如果您覺得餓了，可以在泳池邊的休息吧喝些飲料、吃些糕點休息一會兒。

7. 我們有瑜伽、普拉提和太極課程。

III. Make a dialogue according to the following situation.（創作情景對話）

客人來到健身中心，服務員 B 熱情上前迎接，並詢問先生是否已經預定，客人回答昨天已經電話預定過了，B 詢問客人姓名、房號以及預定時間，客人回答名字叫 Bob，房號

Chapter Five Health & Recreation Service 康樂部

為1008，昨天中午電話預定的今天下午四點過來健身。B查看預訂簿確認客人預定內容無誤後準確登記相關信息，B詢問客人之前是否來過健身房，如果沒有來過可以向其介紹健身房的具體情況，客人回答之前有來過了，不需要介紹，隨後B為客人提供更衣櫃號碼、鑰匙、毛巾等用品。請根據以上情景，創作一篇不少於100個單詞的英文對話。

Unit 2　At the Barbers & Beauty Salon　美容美髮廳

Background（背景知識）

Whether you want a completely new look, an advanced skin treatment or a simple bang trim, please come to our beauty salon. Here you can free your mind and discover yourself! Looking for the perfect massage has never been easier in the beauty salon inside the hotel. The atmosphere provides comfortable, spacious and welcoming environment where you soon forget all your bad moods.

Situationaldialogues（情景對話）

Dialogue 1

B—Barber　G—Mr. Giles

G：Good afternoon.

B：Good afternoon. Can I help you?

G：Yes, I want to have a perm.

B：Would you please wait a moment at the sofa over there?

G：All right. Would it take very long?

B：Maybe another 10 minutes. You might want to read some magazines on the table while you are waiting.

G：What magazines are there to read?

B：You can find the latest fashion and hair style magazine.

G：Oh, that's good.

Translation（譯文）

B—理髮師　G—蓋爾斯先生

G：下午好。

B：下午好，有什麼需要幫忙的嗎？

G：是的，我要燙個頭髮。

B：請在那邊的沙發上等一會兒好嗎？

G：好吧，要很久嗎？

B：也許還要十分鐘。您在等待時可以看看桌上的雜誌。

G：有什麼雜誌呢？

B：您可以找到最新的時尚或髮型的雜誌。

G：那太好了！

Words and expressions（單詞和短語）

barber 理髮師

the barber's 理髮店

perm 燙髮

sofa 沙發

magazine 雜誌

fashion 時尚

hair style 髮型

Dialogue 2

B—Barber　G—Mr. Giles

B：Good morning. Take a seat, please.

G：Thank you. I want a haircut and a shave, please.

B：Very well, and how would you like your haircut, sir?

G：Just a trim, and cut the sides short, but not so much at the back.

B：Nothing off the top?

G：Well, a little off the top.

B：How about the front?

G：Leave the front as it is.

B：OK. Do you want me to trim your moustache?

G：Yes, please.

B：Now have a look, please. Is it all right with you?

G：Yes, it looks good. thanks. And I'd like a shampoo, please.

B：Yes, sir. (After giving the guest a shampoo) Now shall I put on some hair oil or some tonic water?

G：Both, please.

B：Anything else I can do for you?

G：No, thank you. And how much should I pay altogether?

B：That will be fifty yuan.

G：Here you are.

B：Thank you, sir.

Translation（譯文）

B——理髮師　G——蓋爾斯先生

B：早上好。您請坐。

G：謝謝。我想理髮和剃須。

B：好的，先生，您需要怎麼樣的髮式呢？

G：只是修剪一下，兩邊短，但後面不要剪那麼多。

B：頂部不剪嗎？

G：哦，頂部稍微剪短一點。

B：前面要怎麼剪呢？

G：保持原樣。

B：好。您要修剪胡子嗎？

G：好的，拜託。

B：請看看。您看可以嗎？

G：好的，看起來不錯，謝謝。我還想要洗個頭髮。

B：好的，先生。（給客人洗髮後）現在需要加一些髮油或滋補水？

G：都要吧，拜託。

B：還需要什麼服務嗎？

G：不了，謝謝。費用是多少？

B：一共是五十元。

G：給你。

B：謝謝您，先生。

Words and expressions（單詞和短語）

haircut 理髮

shave 刮臉

trim 修剪

moustache 小胡子

shampoo 洗髮

tonic water 滋補水

Dialogue 3

A—Guest　B—Beautician

B: Good afternoon, ma'am. What can I do for you?

A: Good afternoon. I want a facial. But this is the first time I've come here, so can you tell me how you do it?

B: Sure. Most facials start with a thorough cleansing. Then we usually use a toner to invigorate the skin, followed by exfoliation treatment. After that, we'll massage your face and neck with oil to improve the circulation and relieve the tension, followed by a mask to moisturize and soften the skin.

A: That's exactly what I want. How long does it take?

B: There are half-hour and one-hour treatments. The half hour facial costs fifty yuan and the one-hour costs eighty yuan. If you want a make-up, another twenty yuan will do.

A: Good. I'll take the half-hour facial with make-up.

Translation（譯文）

A——客人　B——美容師

B：下午好，女士。我能為你效勞嗎？

A：下午好。我想要做個面部護理。但我第一次來這裡，您能介紹一下怎麼做護理嗎？

B：當然可以。面部護理大都是先徹底清潔。接著通常用爽膚水激活皮膚。然後是脫皮治療。隨後我們用油按摩您的臉和脖子，改善血液循環，緩解緊張。最後是敷面膜滋潤和軟化皮膚。

A：我正想要這個護理。需要多長時間？

B：有半小時和一個小時的治療項目。半小時的面部護理收費50元，一個小時收費80元。如果你想要化妝，再加20元就可以了。

A：好。我要做半小時美容加化妝。

Words and expressions（單詞和短語）

facial 面部用的

treatment 治療

thorough 徹底的

moustache 髭，小鬍子

temple 鬢角

satisfactory 滿意的

toner 調色劑，增色劑

invigorate 滋補，滋潤；使活躍；使健壯

exfoliation 剝落；剝落物

peel 剝（皮）；被剝（或削）去皮

scrub 擦洗；擦淨

massage 給（某人或身體某部位）按摩（或推拿）

circulation 循環，環流；運行

moisturize 給（皮膚、空氣等）增加水分

tonic 滋補的

cleanse 使清潔，清洗

Dialogue 4

A—Guest   B—Manicurist

B：Good afternoon, miss. Have a seat, please.

A：Thank you. I fancy a manicure or a pedicure. How do you charge?

B：We charge 80 yuan for manicure, 30 yuan for pedicure, and 100 yuan for both.

A：Aha. Then I will have both.

B：Very well. What kind of nails would you like? You can have a look at the pictures and pick one.

A：Hum, this one's pretty, but I don't like the paillettes.

B：It's all right. The paillettes are added in the end. I will skip that.

A：Great.

Translation（譯文）

A——客人   B——美甲師

B：下午好，小姐請坐。

A：謝謝，我想做個美甲或者足部修甲，你們怎麼收費？

B：手部美甲是80元，足部修甲是30元，全做的話100元。

A：哈，那我全做。

B：好的，你喜歡哪種指甲？您可以從這些圖片中選一個。

A：嗯，這個不錯，但是我不喜歡亮片。

B：沒關係，亮片是最後加的，我不加就是了。

A：太好了。

Words and expressions（單詞和短語）

fancy 喜歡

manicure 修指甲

pedicure 修腳趾甲

nail 指甲

pretty 漂亮的

paillette 亮片

skip 跳過

Dialogue 5

A—Guest　B—Receptionist

B: Good afternoon, sauna and massage center.

A: Good afternoon. I'd like to know something about your service. What items do you provide?

B: In terms of sauna, we have sauna, steam bath, salt bath and ice bath.

A: What about massage?

B: Thai, Chinese, Japanese massage, hot stone massage, and massages for different parts of the body are all available. And we also offer door-to-door massage service to guests of the hotel.

A: Outstanding. Can you send up a massager here? I am in room 420.

B: Sure. What kind of massage would you like?

A: Back massage. I have been very busy recently, and always feel a pain in the back.

B: In that case, I suggest you have a whole-body massage. It can relieve the pain more effectively than massaging the back only

A: Very well. When will the massager arrive?

B: In five minutes. Do you prefer a male or a female massager?

A: Female, please.

B: The charge is 280 yuan per hour and we only accept cash.

A: All right.

Translation（譯文）

A——客人　B——接待員

B：下午好，桑拿按摩中心。

A：下午好，我想瞭解一下你們的服務。請問你們都有什麼項目？

B：就桑拿而言，我們有干蒸、濕蒸、鹽浴和冰浴。

A：按摩呢？

B：泰式、中式、日式按摩、熱石按摩及全身各處按摩都有。我們還為住店旅客提供上門按摩服務。

A：太棒了，您能派一個按摩師上來嗎，我在420房間。

B：當然。您想做哪種按摩？

A：背部的，我最近很忙，一直背痛。

B：那樣的話，我建議您做一個全身按摩。全身按摩比單純按摩背部更能有效緩解

疼痛。

　　A：好吧，按摩師什麼時候到？

　　B：五分鐘後。您想要男按摩師還是女按摩師？

　　A：女的。

　　B：每小時280元，我們只收現金。

　　A：好的。

Words and expressions（單詞和短語）

sauna 桑拿

massage 按摩

item 項目

in terms of 在……方面

door-to-door 上門的

massager 按摩師

suggest 提議

relieve 緩解

effectively 有效地

I. Translate the following sentences into Chinese.（把下列句子譯成中文）

1. Good afternoon, sir. Take this chair, please.

先生，下午好，請坐這兒。

2. Good afternoon. I want a haircut and a shave, please.

下午好，請替我理髮，並修面。

3. Very well, how would you like your hair cut?

好的，您想剪什麼髮式？

4. Would you keep the same fashion?

照這樣嗎？

5. Please have a look, is it all right?

請看一下，效果好嗎？

6. Would you like to have a shampoo?

您要洗頭嗎？

7. Do you want me to shave off your beard?

胡須要不要給您刮掉？

8. Do you want me to trim your moustache?

要不要把您的胡須修剪一下？

9. How would you like your hair done, madam? Permanent, cold wave, or washed and

dressed?

夫人，您的頭髮式想電燙，冷燙，還是洗一洗做？

10. Can you show me some patterns of hair styles?

您能否給我看一些髮型的式樣？

II. Translate the following sentences into English. （把下列句子譯成英文）

1. 您喜歡在那個位置分頭路？

On which side do you want your parting?

2. 頂上不要剪嗎？

Nothing off the top?

3. 您要不要修面或洗頭？

Would you like a shave or shampoo?

4. 您要修腳指甲嗎？

Would you like a pedicure ?

5. 您比較喜歡什麼樣的髮型？

What hairstyle would you prefer?

6. 這種髮型很適合您的臉型。

It seems to fit your face very well.

7. 夫人，您的頭髮要怎麼處理呢？洗一洗，還是做髮型呢？

Madam, how would you like your hair done? Washed or dressed?

III. Make a dialogue according to the following situation. （創作情景對話）

下午三點四十，客人來到美容美髮廳。服務員 B 上前熱情迎接並詢問客人是美容還是美髮，是否有預約，客人回答是美髮，昨天已經跟托尼理髮師預約好了今天下午四點過來，服務員 B 詢問客人姓名後確認預約單，跟客人說不好意思托尼理髮師現在還在忙，請移步至休息室稍坐片刻，引領客人到休息室就坐後詢問客人是喝茶還是喝水，客人回答溫水就好。請根據以上情景，創作一篇不少於 100 個單詞的英文對話。

參考答案

Chapter One　Front Office 前廳部

Unit 1　Room Reservation　客房預訂

I. Complete the sentences.（補全句子）

1. double 2. difference 3. lake 4. take 5. long 6. leaving 7. to 8. bath 9. available 10. rate 11. per 12. with 13. sounds 14. possible 15. party 16. arrive 17. prefer 18. service 19. suite 20. balcony 21. reservation 22. cancel 23. porter

Unit 2　Reception　登記入住

I. Complete the sentences.（補全句子）

1. waiting 2. charge? 3. including 4. reasonable 5. stay 6. check-in 7. arrive 8. filling 9. advance 10. vacant（spare） 11. recommend 12. room 13. bill 14. departure. 15. How 16. bottom 17. do 18. key card 19. ROOM NUMBER 20. later 21. change 22. key 23. daily 24. sure

Unit 3　Bell Service　應接服務

I. Complete the sentences.（補全句子）

1. with 2. luggage 3. supervisor 4. tips 5. call me 6. view 7. tag 8. bellman 9. slippery 10. packed 11. closet 12. else 13. switch 14. with 15. kind 16. number 17. by the way 18. like 19. spacious 20. wardrobe 21. about 22. amuse 23. walk 24. recreation 25. bowling 26. music 27. laundry 28. daily 29. long 30. open

Unit 4　Telephone Operator　總機服務

I. Complete the sentences.（補全句子）

1. help 2. answer 3. through 4. busy 5. operator 6. dial 7. record 8. country 9. code 10. repeat 11. collect 12. remind 13. right 14. hold 15. through 16. operator 17. disturb

18. message 19. Directory 20. reply 21. cost 22. collect 23. like 24. conference 25. by 26. case 27. wake 28. favour 29. wonder

Unit 5 Business Center 商務中心

I. Complete the sentences.（補全句子）

1. non-smoking 2. water 3. copies 4. lighter 5. original 6. ready. 7. staple 8. top 9. enlarge 10. sides 11. jammed. 12. ink 13. guarantee 14. fax. 15. service 16. minimum 17. code 18. thick 19. copy 20. received 21. font 22. check 23. long 24. Scanning 25. save 26. cash 27. welcome 28. change 29. virus

Unit 6 Dealing with Complaints 處理投訴

I. Complete the sentences.（補全句子）

1. noisy. 2. elevator 3. much 4. sorry 5. apologize. 6. problem 7. spare 8. tomorrow? 9. sleep. 10. know. 11. light 12. brighter 13. back 14. cold 15. details. 16. into 17. mistake 18. assistant 19. trouble 20. send 21. police

Unit 7 Check-out 結帳退房

I. Complete the sentences.（補全句子）

1. bill 2. number 3. used 4. total 5. credit 6. sign 7. today 8. check-out 9. charge 10. account 11. breakfast 12. total 13. meals 14. until 15. cashier 16. currency 17. there 18. difference 19. receipt 20. company

Chapter Two Housekeeping 客房部

Unit 1 Showing Room 客房迎賓服務

I. Complete the sentences.（補全句子）

1. facing 2. mini-bar 3. control 4. flight 5. remote 6. drinkable 7. free 8. at 9. stay 10. facilities. 11. attendant. 12. show 13. like 14. facing 15. outside 16. dial 17. directory 18. channels 19. slippers 20. switch. 21. immediately 22. password 23. original 24. safe 25. Otherwise

參考答案

Unit 2　Room Cleaning　客房清理服務

I. Complete the sentences.（補全句子）

1. time 2. later 3. clean 4. ready 5. between 6. oblige. 7. Turn-down 8. Do Not Disturb 9. continue 10. tired 11. convenient 12. soon 13. earlier 14. Housekeeping 15. clean 16. convenient 17. promise. 18. bathroom 19. towels 20. polishing

Unit 3　Room Service　客房送餐服務

I. Complete the sentences.（補全句子）

1. please 2. time 3. Continental 4. tea 5. many 6. away. 7. ordered. 8. besides 9. bill 10. enjoy 11. prepare 12. sign 13. lunch 14. Room 15. pour 16. drinks 33. take 18. with 19. at 20. until 21. there 22. menu 23. birthday 24. prefer 25. past 26. brought 27. butter 28. done 29. glass 30. plates 31. serve

Unit 4　Laundry Service　洗衣服務

I. Complete the sentences.（補全句子）

1. laundry 2. noon 3. folder 4. pick up 5. minutes. 6. shirts 7. right 8. pressed 9. form 10. drawer 11. starched 12. shrink 13. understand 14. pick 15. deliver 16. bed 17. dry-cleaned 18. facilities 19. mending 20. stain 21. sauce 22. guarantee 23. extra 24. refund 25. inconvenience 26. wear 27. collar 28. damaged 29. form 30. pairs 31. pocket 32. missing. 33. button 34. check

Unit 5　Emergencies　突發事件處理

I. Complete the sentences.（補全句子）

1. where 2. hear 3. call 4. ambulance 5. fire 6. typhoon 7. exit 8. recover 9. office 10. remember 11. calm 12. damage

Unit 6　Other Housekeeping Service　客房其他服務

I. Complete the sentences.（補全句子）

1. woken 2. computer 3. soon 4. experienced 5. shop 6. repair 7. replaced 8. nightstand. 9. another 10. luggage. 11. electrician 12. repaired

Chapter Three   Food and Beverage   餐飲部

Unit 1   Reservation   預訂餐臺

I. Translate the following sentences into Chinese.（把下列句子譯成中文）

1. 什麼時候，先生？
2. 您何時光臨？
3. 你們一共幾個人？
4. 您為誰預定？
5. 可以告訴我您的姓名嗎？
6. 感謝您來電話。
7. 對不起，先生，晚上7點以前的餐桌都訂滿了，8點的行嗎？
8. 只有晚上8點以後才有空位。
9. 您想坐在哪裡？
10. 我們期盼您的光臨。
11. 我們會安排好一切的。

II. Translate the following sentences into English.（把下列句子譯成英文）

1. Do I need a reservation?
2. I'd like to reserve a table for three.
3. We are a group of six.
4. We'll come around eight o'clock.
5. How can I get there?
6. I'd like to reserve a table for two at seven tonight.
7. I'm sorry. We have so many guests this evening.
8. How long is the wait?
9. Nine o'clock should be O. K.
10. What do you have for today's special?
11. We'd like a table with a view of garden.
12. Do you have a dress code?
13. Could the ladies wear formal dresses?
14. No jeans, please.

Unit 2　Receiving Guests　迎客服務

I. Translate the following sentences into Chinese.（把下列句子譯成中文）

1. 晚上好，先生。歡迎光臨。您預定了嗎？

2. 這邊請。

3. 您是兩人嗎？

4. 很抱歉，現在沒有空桌子了。

5. 對不起，那張桌子已被預定了。

6. 請在休息室（大廳）等幾分鐘好嗎？一有空位我馬上通知您。

7. 請坐。給您菜單。我一會兒就回來為您點菜。

II. Translate the following sentences into English.（把下列句子譯成英文）

1. Your table is ready now.

2. Do you have a breakfast voucher?

3. Sorry, there is no table available right now.

4. Would you mind sharing a table with that lady?

5. Yes, sir. I can change a table in the corner for you.

6. I'm very sorry, that table has been reserved.

7. If you want that one tomorrow or some other days, I will have it reserved for you.

Unit 3　Taking Orders for Western Food　西餐點單

I. Translate the following sentences into Chinese.（把下列句子譯成中文）

1. 餐廳是否有供應素食餐？

2. 是否有中文菜單？

3. 在用晚餐前想喝些什麼嗎？

4. 餐廳有些什麼餐前酒？

5. 可否讓我看看酒單？

6. 我可以點杯酒嗎？

7. 餐廳有哪幾類酒？

8. 我想點當地出產的酒。

9. 我想要喝法國紅酒。

10. 是否可建議一些不錯的酒？

11. 我可以點餐了嗎？

12. 餐廳最特別的菜式是什麼？

13. 餐廳有今日特餐嗎？

14. 我可以點與那份相同的餐嗎？

15. 我想要一份開胃菜與排餐（魚餐）。

16. 我正在節食中。

17. 我必須避免含油脂（鹽份/糖份）的食物。

II. Translate the following sentences into English.（把下列句子譯成英文）

1. May I take your order now?

2. What would you like to drink?

3. How would you like your steak, well-done, medium or rare?

4. How would you like your egg?

5. Would you like to try our House Specialty, Mapo Tofu?

6. Would you like anything else?

7. Your order will be ready very soon.

8. Here's your meal.

9. Enjoy your meal, sir.

10. Would you like your coffee to be served first or after the dishes?

Unit 4　Taking Orders for Chinese Food　中餐點菜

I. Translate the following sentences into Chinese.（把下列句子譯成中文）

1. 我們有套餐提供。

2. 我們提供自助餐，你可以選擇你們喜歡的東西。

3. 我想向您推薦檸檬鴨。

4. 這道菜相當美味。

5. 要不要試一試廚師長的推薦菜？

6. 一切都滿意吧？

7. 給您帳單。請查看一下。您可以簽單，酒店會在您離店時一起給您結帳。

II. Translate the following sentences into English.（把下列句子譯成英文）

1. Welcome to our restaurant. Are you here for the wedding banquet of Mr. John?

2. May I serve the dishes now?

3. Please enjoy your meal.

4. Today's special is Mapo Tofu with a 40% discount.

5. This bottle of wine is finished. Would you like one more?

6. May I separate the dish for you?

7. Do you care for something a little stronger? If you prefer something milder, you may try some ricewine available here.

8. Are you satisfied with the meal, sir?

9. Excuse me, madam. Shall I change a new side plate for you?

10. The charge for a 300-person-dinner party is RMB 15,000 yuan, excluding beverages.

11. I am sorry, sir. Our restaurant is fully booked on the evening of 14th.

12. Food is usually served from the left and beverages are served from the right.

13. For set menus, the expenses per head range from RMB 100 yuan, RMB 150 yuan to RMB 180 yuan. Which would you prefer?

Unit 5　At the Bar　酒吧服務

I. Translate the following sentences into Chinese.（把下列句子譯成中文）

1. 您要喝點什麼？

2. 現在，在就餐前不來點飲料嗎？

3. 跟往常一樣，先生？

4. 要不要加冰？

5. 此葡萄酒是1990年釀製成的。

6.（送上酒時說）慢慢享用，先生。

7. 您想不想試試中國的酒呢？

8. 這是我們的酒水牌。我們的藏酒非常豐富。

9. 先生，再來同樣的一杯（瓶）嗎？

10. 贈送的食物當然是不收費的。

II. Translate the following sentences into English.（把下列句子譯成英文）

1. I'm sorry, sir. That's our minimum charge—two drinks at 90 RMB each, plus 10% service charge.

2. How about a Fruit Juice Cup? That has：champagne, dark rum, orange juice, lemon juice, pineapple juice, sugar and ginger ale in it?

3. How about a Manhattan? It is a classic drink：Canadian whiskey, vermouth and angostura bitter.

4. The Fruit Cocktail has orange, grapefruit, passion fruit, lime, mango and pineapple juice, with just a little kiwi syrup in it.

5. We don't have any draught beer. We only have bottled beer.

6. The Hawaii Surfer is similar to Magic Island, with coconut, pineapple and orange sorbet.

7. What's your pleasure this evening, Mr. Brown? Your usual beer?

8. It's a「Pousse Cafe」or「Rainbow Cocktail」, and it is made from several liqueurs. It looks like a rainbow.

9. Buying beer by the pitcher is cheaper than buying it by the glass.

10. I'm sorry but I can't serve you since you're intoxicated.

Chapter Four　Conferences　會務

Unit 1　Conference service　會議服務

I. Translate the following sentences into Chinese.（把下列句子譯成中文）

1. 請您說得再具體一點，好嗎？
2. 請問多少人參加會議？
3. 先生，請問將有多少客人出席呢？
4. 請問會議類型？
5. 這個活動是正式的還是非正式的？
6. 您希望招待會幾點開始呢？
7. 這個宴會您考慮是全天的還是半天的呢？

II. Translate the following sentences into English.（把下列句子譯成英文）

1. Will the banquet be an indoor or outdoor function?
2. I'll send you details of our various function rooms.
3. Would you like our set wedding lunch?
4. Would you like me to fax you our range of menus?
5. I'll include details of prices per head and the floor plans.
6. We have several multifunctional rooms of various sizes.
7. Our Lotus Room can accommodate up to 300 people.
8. Wireless microphones and clip-on microphone are provided.
9. I'll fax it to you before the end of the day.

Chapter Five　Health & Recreation Service　康樂部

Unit One　At the recreation center　健身中心

I. Translate the following sentences into Chinese.（把下列句子譯成中文）

1. 您可以去我們這的恒溫游泳池去泡一泡，游泳也是提高身體素質和保持體形的最佳方法之一。

2. 我們有裝備完善的健身房，擁有最新的消遣運動器械，如供鍛煉用的腳踏車、舉重器械及肋木之類的運動器材。

3. 健身器材使用後請擦拭乾淨。

4. 您可以免費使用救生圈和獨立更衣室。

5. 您使用那臺設備時需要協助嗎？

II. Translate the following sentences into English.（把下列句子譯成英文）

1. How often do you work out?

2. Push it. Give me five more reps!

3. This exercise will help build your shoulders.

4. If you feel burned out now, it is good to stop.

5. If you strain a muscle or hurt your back, then you won't be able to exercise for a couple weeks.

6. If you feel hungry, you can relax with soft drinks and some pastries at the poolside bar.

7. We offer yoga, Pilates, and Tai Chi classes.

Unit Two   At the Barbers & Beauty Salon   美容美髮廳

I. Translate the following sentences into Chinese.（把下列句子譯成中文）

1. 先生，下午好，請坐這。

2. 下午好，請替我理髮，並修面。

3. 好的，您想剪什麼髮式？

4. 照這樣嗎？

5. 請看一下，效果好嗎？

6. 您要洗頭嗎？

7. 胡須要不要給您刮掉？

8. 要不要把您的胡須修剪一下？

9. 夫人，您的頭髮式想電燙、冷燙，還是洗一洗做？

10. 您能否給我看一些髮型的式樣？

II. Translate the following sentences into English.（把下列句子譯成英文）

1. On which side do you want your parting?

2. Nothing off the top?

3. Would you like a shave or shampoo?

4. Would you like a pedicure?

5. What hairstyle would you prefer?

6. It seems to fit your face very well.

7. Madam, how would you like your hair done? Washed or dressed?

Appendix: Extended Reading Materials on Hotel Reviews[①]
(附錄:關於酒店評論的泛讀材料)

Park City Marriott

The hotel is located in the Prospector Square in Park City, approximately two miles from Park City Main Street and the Park City Mountain Resort. There are a couple of shops and restaurants in walking distance, but you'd be best served with a car if you're staying here. The hotel is served by the free Park City Winter Bus, which stops directly in front of the hotel.

The hotel has 4 floors with 192 guestrooms. It is built around a indoor pool atrium — half the rooms face outside, and half the rooms face inside to the pool. If you're looking for a room that you can get some fresh air, ask for a room that faces outside.

The hotel lobby has a cozy feel to it with a few couches placed in front of a large fireplace. Guests are provided with complimentary cookies, hot chocolate, and apple-cider in the afternoon (around 4 pm). There's a coffee shop selling Starbucks coffee, two restaurants, and a ski-shop also on the lobby level.

Breakfast for Gold and Platinum members is provided in the Concierge Lounge 7 days a week from 6:30 am-9 am. The concierge lounge is quite small, and can get crowded at the 「peak」 8:30 am breakfast time.

The room itself was a pretty standard comfy Marriott room. My only complaint is that the air conditioning didn't really work in my room at all — so it was quite hot. I tried opening the balcony door to get some fresh air, but those free Park City buses drove by every 15 minutes, which made my sleeping not so easy.

Hyatt Escala Lodge in Park City Utah

The Hyatt Escala Lodge is located at the top of the Canyons Park City Resort. There's a small

---

① 全文摘自網路,有改動。原文網址: http://yelloww.net/category/hotels/

ski lift right next door to the hotel. It's just a short five minute's walk to the Canyon's main 「village」 and main lifts.

The Hyatt Escala Lodge is composed of three buildings. Two of the buildings are connected via inside corridor. The main lobby is in the Wasatch Building. Valet Parking and Free Underground Self Parking are available.

The lobby has a nice seating area in front of a fireplace. Also in the lobby is a quick-serve restaurant and the hotel's sit down restaurant. There is a small 「business center」 with one computer. Next to the elevators is a 「DVD-Now」 kiosk where you can pickup free DVDs to watch in-room.

The gym is on the smallish side, but it is very clean and well equipped with windows facing out to the pool area. There is a very nice heated pool and two heated spas. Sitting in the big round hot spa was one of the highlights of my stay. The gym area also includes a Sauna and a Steam Room.

We stayed in room 338A, of the middle building. It was on the top floor, with loft style ceilings. The room itself was a nice large size. Two comfortable beds. A pretty lame excuse of a desk, but I assume most people aren't here for a work. There was a 「mini-kitchen」 area with a Sub-Zero mini-fridge, microwave, and sink. The bathroom was large with a separate tub and glassed in shower. Overall a very nice room.

I'd definitely consider staying here again on a trip to Park City.

Rome Marriott Grand Flora Hotel in Rome, Italy

The Rome Marriott Grand Flora Hotel is located on Via Veneto, about a 7-minute walk (uphill) from the Barberini Subway station. To get to the hotel I took the Leonardo Express Airport Train (14 Euro) to Termini Station, and then walked (about 20 minutes) to the hotel. Via Veneto is one of the most famous streets in Rome and is home to quite a few upscale hotels. The Marriott has a perfect location at the top of the hill, so there are superb views from the rooftop restaurant.

The hotel has 150 rooms on 7 floors. The hotel is built around a central courtyard. If you want a quiet room, ask for one facing the courtyard. I had a room facing the courtyard and I honestly didn't hear a single sound from outside my room. I booked a 「smaller room」 from the website (one twin bed). But as Platinum member I was upgraded to a slightly larger room with two twin beds (look like a king bed because they are right next to each other). Even so, the room was still on the 「small」 side, but very functional. The A/C worked well, the windows opened, and the bathroom had great water pressure. What else can you ask for in a hotel? Oh… and it had a heated towel rack!

Funaya Onsen Hotel in Matsuyama, Japan

Funaya is a traditional Japanese style Onsen (hot-spring) hotel with 68 rooms. It is located in Matsuyama Japan, in the Dogo Onsen neighborhood. If you are driving, the hotel provides free valet parking. If you are taking the train, it is a short 5 minute walk from the Dogo Onsen train station. It is also very near (5 minute walk) to the historic Dogo Onsen public bath.

The hotel is composed of two buildings, the one with the lobby and most of the hotel rooms, and a second building that has the hot spring baths. The two buildings are connected by an elevated/enclosed bridge that crosses over a stream and a Japanese garden. The Onsens are located on the 2nd and 3rd floor of the other building. Men and Women alternate between which bath they use depending upon the time of the day. Outside of the 2nd floor bath is a nice resting area with complimentary ice tea.

You can book the room with or without dinner. We booked the room rate with the 「Fusion」 dinner. While the food was good, from beginning to end it took about 2 hours. They bring each course one at a time, so be prepared to do a bit of waiting for your food to be freshly cooked and prepared. The below video is of the dinner:

The room itself was one of the largest rooms that I've ever stayed at in Japan. It had a large main 「sleeping」 room (where you sleep on futons), a room off to the side where they would slide the table from the main room when you are sleeping, a sitting room by the window, a dressing room, and a 「3-room」 bathroom (toilet, sink, bath).

Overall I really enjoyed my stay at Funaya. The Onsen was great, the room was quiet, and the service was excellent. It wasn't cheap, but it was well worth it!

Renaissance Naruto Resort in Naruto, Japan

The Renaissance Naruto Resort is located on the coast in Naruto, very close to the famous Naruto whirlpools (about a 5-10 minute drive). If you are planning to stay here, I would highly recommend a rental car, as there isn't much of anything within walking distance of the hotel. The hotel has a total of 208 guestrooms, all of which are oceanfront. There are beaches on both sides of the hotel, but directly in front of the hotel are just some concrete blocks.

The property has two different Onsens, Japanese Hot-Spring Baths, one on the first floor, and the other on the eighth floor with a bit of an ocean-view. Outside is a small kidney bean shaped swimming pool. Other interesting things on property include 「Naruto Fishland」 where you can fish in a small man-made pond, or you can pet some turtles.

As a platinum member I received free breakfast, with a choice of the downstairs 「western」 restaurant, or the upstairs Japanese buffet. I picked the Japanese buffet because that's where everybody seemed to be. It was pretty good, just don't expect pancakes or anything of that sort :). There are a couple of other restaurants on property, including a Japanese BBQ.

The room itself was clean and quiet. It had 2 beds, a little sofa, desk. Two bottles of complementary water, two fans, and a Renaissance Naruto mascot 「zipper pull」 were provided on the coffee table. In the dresser underneath the television they provided the Yukatas, to be worn when you visit the Onsen.

Overall I really enjoyed my stay, and would highly recommend the Renaissance Naruto Resort for anyone visiting Naruto.

Hilton Hawaiian Village in Honolulu, Hawaii

The Hilton Hawaiian Village is truly a mega-hotel — it's the largest hotel in the Hilton Chain and the 18th largest hotel in the world with over 3,300 rooms. The hotel is located on the North-Western edge of Waikiki, close to the Ala Moana Shopping Center. To walk from the hotel to the 「center」 of Waikiki takes about 15-20 minutes.

The hotel has six tower buildings, six pools, 90 shops, 20 restaurants, a lagoon, and a beach. So as you can tell — there's a ton of stuff to see and do on this property. They also feature a nightly Luau Sun-Thurs, and fireworks shows on Friday nights at 7:45 p.m. For the best view of the fireworks show, pay $20 to watch the 「Rockin' Rainbow Revue」 at the Super Pool at 7 p.m. on Friday. You'll have a seat by the pool, and the fireworks start immediately after the show.

There's a big parking garage in the middle of the property, so self parking is pretty easy. They advertise a rate of $27/night for self parking, but I was only charged $18/night for parking. Valet is of course also available.

The lobby is this not-really-indoor / not-really-outdoor space. It's basically a covered area with a roof but no walls. Check-in for the most of the resort occurs at this central lobby, but some of the towers have their own check-in desks.

As a Hilton Honors Gold+ member, you have the option of of 1,000 points (one time) or a $10 food credit per day per person. The food credit is really the way to go. You don't have to spend the food credit all in one day as it is a cumulative credit.

We got a room on the 31st floor of the Tapa Tower. The views were really awesome from that level, but the wait for elevators was a huge time-sink. Going up to our room we regularly had to wait 「in-line」 for multiple elevators before we could get in one to go up. Going up to the room to get something we forgot and coming back down to ground level could be 15-minutes of time wasted.

The room itself was a typical Hilton room, nothing particularly noteworthy or outstanding about it.

JW Marriott Las Vegas in Nevada

I booked just a standard rate at this hotel – something relatively inexpensive in the ＄100 range, and as a Platinum member was upgraded to the awesome two bedroom suite. I think this room is bigger than my house! The room had two full bedrooms, three bathrooms, a living room + dining room area, a full bar, and a wrap-around balcony.

I did shoot this video a couple of years ago, so I imagine they may have upgraded the 「tube」 TVs to flat panel televisions by now, but the video should give you a great idea of the room itself.

Las Vegas Marriott in Las Vegas, Nevada

The Las Vegas Marriott is located across the street from the Las Vegas Convention, and about two blocks from the North end of the Las Vegas Strip, near the Encore and Riveria hotels. The Las Vegas Marriott is a 17 story 278 room hotel. I like to stay here because there is convenient parking, that you can get to the garage quickly from your room. In most Las Vegas hotels the parking garage is a 20 minute hike from the actual hotel rooms!

This hotel used to be a 「Marriott Suites」 so most of the rooms are 「suite style」 with a separate living room and bedroom. The hotel was remodeled a few years ago when they did the switchover from the 「Marriott Suites」 to the just the regular 「Marriott」 property. There is no concierge lounge here, but gold and platinum guests do get a free full breakfast at the restaurant in the lobby.

The rooms here are all very quiet due to the 「suite」 design. I found the bedding to be comfortable, the Air Conditioning to be cold, and the sleep quality to be good. What more can you ask for?

THE hotel at Mandalay Bay in Las Vegas

The V Suite is given it's name because they are the rooms at the edge of the 「V」 of the hotel. Each floor of the hotel has four V Suites.

When you come in to the room, immediately to one side is a little guest bathroom, with a toilet and a sink. The room is divided in to two main areas, the living room portion, and the bedroom portion. Inside the living room was a sofa that seats three people, a sofa chair, coffee table, desk, flat panel TV, and mini-bar. The bedroom was composed of a king size bed (all V

Suites only have one king bed), flat panel television, and another sofa chair. The bedroom is really a neat shape (you have to see the video for that). The bathroom was very large with two sinks, a separate bathtub and shower, and of course a television!

The windows of the hotel have a very interesting 「Gold」 color, visible from the outside, AND the inside of the room. The windows don't really open, but they do have a little vent thing that you can slide over to get a tiny bit of fresh air.

Overall I really enjoyed my stay in the V Suite and would consider it again for a future trip to Las Vegas!

Hotel Monterey Osaka

This hotel is located a 5 minute walk from the Sakura-bashi exit of the JR Osaka Station, directly across the street from the train tracks. The close proximity to the train station is good, and bad. Good because it's very convenient for sightseeing, as you can go anywhere from Osaka station. Bad because the train tracks are very loud, and if you are a light sleeper, beware!

The Hotel Monterey Osaka is a very odd juxtaposition of things. Coming from the USA, it was definitely odd to be staying in a Vienna Palace themed hotel in Japan. Especially since our last vacation trip was to Vienna. That being said, this hotel does a good job of recreating that European feeling… all the way down to the 「historic looking」 elevators, staircases, revolving doors, and replica 14th century stone chapel. Oh that last bit, yes there is a replica 14th Century Chapel on the 8th floor of the building. And it's a perfect replica, all the way down to the steps and roof. It's the whole chapel building, except it's on the 8th floor of this hotel. Again, weird.

How was the room itself? In a word — small. I've stayed in quite a few Japanese hotels, so I'm used to small. It wasn't tiny… but it was definitely small. The double room is OK for one person. It's too crammed in for two people though. There's really no place to open a suitcase anywhere in the room except for on top of the bed. On the plus side, the room was clean, and had 「black-out」 wooden shades over the windows. So the room could get really dark, but because of the proximity to the train tracks, it could never get that quiet. With the air purifier on high, and air conditioning on high, I could drown out the sound of the trains enough to sleep, but the sound of the train rumbling was always there somewhere in the background.

If you like trains, and aren't bothered by train noise, this could be a good choice. However if you're a light sleeper like me, then pick someplace else a bit further away from the tracks.

JR Hotel Clement Takamatsu

This hotel is located adjacent to the JR Takamatsu Station. You can walk from the station to the hotel in 1 minute via an outdoor covered walkway. The hotel has a large, modern, open lobby. On the ground floor of the hotel surrounding the lobby is the lobby bar, a lunch/dinner buffet restaurant, a bakery, a wedding salon, and the hotel gift shop. Check-in itself was easy as the hotel front desk spoke English well.

I booked a Hollywood Suite from Rakuten at a rate of 20,000 Yen per night. We were given a room in the 18th floor, with some incredible views of the harbor. The room itself was very large for Japanese standards which was a welcome change since I just came from a hotel in Osaka that had very very tiny rooms. The amenities inside the room included two twin beds, desk, chaise lounge, arm chair, flat and of course a flat panel TV. Some 「unique」items in the room were a pants press (to keep your pants wrinkle free), an air purifier, and a hot water kettle. The bathroom was also very large, with a full bath and separate shower.

I found my sleep quality in the room to be very good. The room was quiet, the air conditioning was cold, and the beds were comfortable.

For our first day of travelling in Takamatsu we rented a bicycle for 200 Yen from the municipal bike rental which is in the garage just outside the hotel. For our second day of touring we rented a car, and parked it in the hotel garage overnight for 1,000 Yen.

Overall I had an excellent stay at this hotel and would highly recommend it.

Vail Marriott Mountain Resort and Spa

The Vail Marriott is located on the West side of Vail in Lionshead village. I drove in from Denver on a Saturday morning and the 110 mile drive took about 3 hours due to the ski-resort bound traffic on the I-70. The Vail Marriott is a short 5 minute or so walk to the Eagle Bahn Gondola.

Arrival at the hotel was very convenient as the valet immediately approach our car, whisked our bags away, and led us to the front desk. It was about 12:30p.m. and our room wasn't yet ready. The front desk took down my cell phone number and offered to call me once the room was available. In about an hour I got a friendly call letting me know the room was available.

As a Marriott Platinum member I was offered a welcome gift of points, or a $10 food & beverage credit. I took the $10 food credit to use at the in hotel Starbucks later. Starbucks is certainly the cheapest breakfast option inside the hotel (it's located on the 2nd floor of the lobby, open until 11am). The regular breakfast at the hotel is extremely expensive! Pancakes and eggs is like $30. Some other breakfast options that I'd recommend in Lionshead village are The Little Diner (a block away from the hotel), and Tavern on the Square in front of the Eagle Bahn Gondola.

Once we checked in the room, the bell-boy brought our bags up in just a few minutes. The room overall was fairly small but comfortable. The bathroom looked to have been recently remodeled and was easily the nicest part of the room. Sleep quality was pretty good. It was quiet, and we kept the balcony door open so that brought in plenty of cool fresh air.

Since this is considered a 「resort」 hotel, there is no concierge lounge or free breakfast. As a resort it also has a $30/day resort fee. The resort gets you free internet, 4 bottles of water, ski valet, and 2 free welcome cocktails.

There are 2 swimming pools, and 2 hot-hubs. One of the sets of pool/hottub is outside, and the other set is inside (basement level). On the ground floor of the hotel by the pool there is a huge sporting goods store. A great place to pick up those last minute items.

Parking is 100% Valet Parking. $32 per night in the winter, $21 per night in the summer. Performance of the valet was always excellent. I never had to wait more than 10 minutes for my car. The free Vail bus stops directly in front of the hotel, and arrives every 10 minutes or so. A pretty nice touch is they have a heat lamp directly above where you wait for the bus so it's not too cold.

Overall I'd recommend the Vail Marriott if you've got points to redeem. I'm not sure that I'd pay the rack rate of $500-$700/night during the winter months though — seems a bit steep to me… but I guess it is Vail!

Conrad Singapore Hotel

The Conrad is located in the Marina Bay district just a short 2-minute walk from the Promenade MRT Station. A great location for business, or being a tourist. There is also a huge supermarket in the basement of the adjacent Suntec City plaza.

I checked in at about 2:00 a.m. … overall check-in was very efficient even at this late hour. As a Hilton Gold member I was upgraded to a 「business」 room which included $20 of free laundry credit. They asked when my checkout was (2 days later at 5:00a.m.) and they notified me that they could pack a complimentary 「to go」 breakfast for early departing guests. I didn't take them up on this offer, but it was a nice touch.

The room was very nicely appointed. The room was quite, had good air conditioning, and a comfy bed. Of course there was the complimentary Conrad Singapore teddy bear and rubber ducky. A plate of fresh fruit and chocolates was also placed in the room.

Overall a great hotel — I'd highly recommend a stay here if you're planning a trip to Singapore.

Singapore Marriott

The Singapore Marriott is located in Singapore's shopping Mecca known as Orchard Road. It is a very convenient spot for being a tourist as the hotel is situated directly above the Orchard Road MRT station. There's also a great food-court located across the street on level B4 of the Ion Orchard shopping mall.

The room itself was small with two beds, but it was clean, well maintained, and most importantly for me, quiet.

As a Platinum member I was provided access to the lounge, and also a choice of a full breakfast buffet in the restaurant on the ground floor. If you'll be staying here, definitely take the breakfast in the restaurant.

Conrad Macao Cotai Central

This room was truly awesome and I was upgraded to it as a Gold member! Huge living room, media room, and a ridiculously large bathroom. Highly recommended!

The hotel itself is located in the Cotai Sands Complex which is a complex of three hotels (Holiday Inn, Sheraton, Conrad) that share a common casino/shopping mall/eateries. The complex was recently completed in 2012 and is located directly across the street from the Venetian and the City of Dreams.

The Conrad provides a free shuttle bus from the Taipa Ferry Terminal. I took the Cotai Water Jet Ferry from Hong Kong to Macau which was a pleasant trip. At the ferry terminal there was a staff member from the Conrad holding a sign that said「Conrad.」I identified myself to the staff member and she walked me to the shuttle bus. The shuttle bus would not have been easy to find without the help of the Conrad staff member.

It's pretty easy to get to the old town of Macau via a taxi from the Conrad. Taxi's were about \$10 to the Historic Centre, and were readily available at the lobby entrance of the Conrad. For those that are extremely cheap, there is also a free shuttle bus that runs to the Historic Centre from the City of Dreams hotel complex next door.

Conrad Hong Kong

Overall a pretty decent room, but the only「spectacular」thing in my mind about the room was the view. Otherwise I'd just consider it to be a really nice Hilton room. As a Gold Member staying on the weekend I was not upgraded to the Executive Floor, but received free breakfast in the restaurant instead. The breakfast was just「OK.」I also stayed at the JW Marriott on this same trip and MUCH preferred the JW Marriott over the Conrad. The rooms at the JW were nicer, and the breakfast at the JW was way better.

JW Marriott Hong Kong Hotel

The JW Marriott is located on Hong Kong Island within a short walk (<5min) of the Admirality MTR station via underground tunnel. The hotel is also situated directly above the Pacific Place shopping mall. For those that want to do some grocery shopping, there is a grocery store in the basement level of the Pacific Place shopping mall. Overall it's an excellent location for tourists or business travelers.

To get to the hotel from the airport I took the Airport Express train to the final 「Hong Kong」 stop which takes about 20 minutes from the airport. From the airport train station I took the complimentary Airport Express Shuttle Bus — H1. The ride on the H1 shuttle took about 7 minutes to reach the JW Marriott… very easy.

Upon arrival at the JW Marriott the bell staff grabbed my luggage and directed me to the check-in desk. Check in was easy and the front desk staff indicated they had booked me in to a 「quiet room」 per my request, and I was upgraded to the Executive level. Once my check-in paperwork was completed, I was escorted to my room by the staff-member that processed my check-in AND the bell-boy that had my luggage.

The check-in assistant showed off the various bells and whistles in the room, like how the curtains open by the push of a button, while the bell-boy set my luggage up on a stand. After being in the room for about 10 minutes, housekeeping rang the doorbell with a special 「welcome gift」 of hot-tea and a fruit plate. The housekeeping staff that brought the tea also poured it in to a cup before leaving.

As a Gold/Platinum Marriott Rewards member I was given the option of breakfast in the lounge of the Marriott Cafe. Definitely take breakfast in the Marriott Cafe. It's easily the best Marriott breakfast I've ever had. Not only is the food awesome, and the staff is super attentive and polished.

The room itself was very nice… my words won't do it justice, so just watch the video.

I also stayed at the Conrad Hong Kong on this trip… and for those that are debating between the JW or the Conrad, I'd highly recommend the JW Marriott. I felt the rooms at the JW were nicer, the staff was more attentive, and the breakfast at the JW was FAR superior to that at the Conrad. Yes, the Conrad has better views of the harbor from the guest rooms, but the JW Marriott also has an excellent view of the harbor from the Concierge Lounge if your room doesn't have one.

Overall I had an excellent stay at this hotel and would highly recommend it to anyone going to Hong Kong.

Daiichi Takimotokan hotel in Noboribetsu, Hokkaido, Japan

Getting to the hotel couldn't have been easier since we took the hotel's bus from the Sapporo JR Train Station to the hotel. Make sure that you reserve the bus in advance though! Note: When we called the hotel to make bus reservations, nobody spoke English. So I might suggest reserving through their website or e-mail.

Checking in was easy, and the check in staff spoke English and gave us English language maps and information on the property. We booked a Japanese style room in the newest tower on property. The lady that brought us to our room spoke English and explained the various amenities of the room. She also brought me a「XL」Yukata and sandals since I'm a big American guy. The room itself was plain, but nice. In addition to the usual large tatami area with table, there was a seating area next to the window with a cool view of the valley.

The Onsen, also known as the Grand Bath, is one of the biggest Onsens that I've been to in all of Japan. It is two stories and features seven different types and temperatures of water. The Grand Bath is truly grand, though it is a relatively old building. I also found it to be a it of a bummer that most of the bath's were inside. Only two of the baths were outside, which is where I spent the majority of my time because I really like to be in the Onsen outside in the fresh air. After the time in the Onsen there is some very tasty Iced Tea server in the locker room. You should definitely try it!

The dinner buffet was also excellent! It's probably one of the best buffets that I've had a hotel in Japan and definitely the most filling meal that I had during my trip to Hokkaido.

The area, Noboribetsu, is quite a little touristy town. After checking in to the hotel you might consider to take a quick「hike」over to Hell Valley, where the Hot Spring water is bubbling up from the ground. It's a cool attraction, and lots of tour buses drop people off there just to view it. During certain seasons the path to the Hot Spring is light up at night which makes for a fun night-time walk as well.

Overall I had a wonderful stay at this hotel and would highly recommend a stay at this hotel!

Hyatt Regency Lake Tahoe

The Hyatt Regency Lake Tahoe is located on the Northeast portion of the lake in the small town of Incline Village, Nevada. The hotel is located on the shore of Lake Tahoe and the rooms on high floors of the main building have beautiful views of the lake through the pine three. With the exception of the Hyatt, there really a whole lot going on in Incline Village itself. But the good news is the Hyatt has quite a few amenities on it's own property including a casino, three restaurants, a bar, a spa, and an action sports store. Just be aware that the Hyatt is at least a 30 minute drive to any ski or snowboarding destinations.

The hotel has a neat「lodgey」feeling about it and doesn't look like your typical「cookie cutter」large chain hotel. The furniture in the hotel rooms all appear to be made from「natural looking」wood (see the video for what I mean).

We had dinner at the Lone Eagle Grille which has views directly out to the shores of the lake. The restaurant has a really neat「mountain lodge」atmosphere, and the food is pretty good. The cream of mushroom soup and the black rice risotto were excellent, but the price is certainly high. The bill for two at the restaurant came out to be about $100.

Self Parking and Valet Parking are both available at the hotel, and are「included」in the $25/day resort fee. Something comforting to know during snow is the hotel valet will also sell and install snow chains on your car for $80 ($50 to buy the chains, $30 to install).

Overall, I had a great stay at the Hyatt Regency Lake Tahoe, and would recommend it to other travelers that are planning a trip to the area.

國家圖書館出版品預行編目（CIP）資料

酒店服務英語簡明教程 / 覃始龍 著. -- 第一版.
-- 臺北市：財經錢線文化，2020.05
　　面；　公分
POD版

ISBN 978-957-680-405-2(平裝)

1.英語 2.旅館業 3.會話

805.188　　　　109005512

書　　名：酒店服務英語簡明教程
作　　者：覃始龍 著
發 行 人：黃振庭
出 版 者：財經錢線文化事業有限公司
發 行 者：財經錢線文化事業有限公司
E-mail：sonbookservice@gmail.com
粉 絲 頁：　　　　　網　址：
地　　址：台北市中正區重慶南路一段六十一號八樓815室
8F.-815, No.61, Sec. 1, Chongqing S. Rd., Zhongzheng Dist., Taipei City 100, Taiwan (R.O.C.)
電　　話：(02)2370-3310　傳　真：(02) 2388-1990
總 經 銷：紅螞蟻圖書有限公司
地　　址：台北市內湖區舊宗路二段 121 巷 19 號
電　　話：02-2795-3656　傳真：02-2795-4100　　網址：
印　　刷：京峯彩色印刷有限公司（京峰數位）

本書版權為西南財經大學出版社所有授權崧博出版事業股份有限公司獨家發行電子書及繁體書繁體字版。若有其他相關權利及授權需求請與本公司聯繫。

定　　價：280 元
發行日期：2020 年 05 月第一版

◎ 本書以 POD 印製發行